MISSION TO THE MOON

by

Lester del Rey

THUNDERCHILD PUBLISHING
Huntsville, Alabama

MISSION TO THE MOON

Copyright © 1956 by Lester del Rey (renewed 1984)

Published by agreement with Wildside Press LLC and John Gregory Betancourt.

ISBN-13: 978-1517631246
ISBN-10: 1517631246

Published by Thunderchild Publishing
1898 Shellbrook Drive
Huntsville, AL 35806

Cover illustration by Alex Schomburg.

Table of Contents

Dedication

To

DOUGLAS *and* KAREN

who may see it happen!

Dreams That Became Realities

MANY PEOPLE believe that the conquest of space began when President Eisenhower announced that the United States would send tiny satellites up to circle the Earth in 1957 or 1958. Actually, the real conquest of space began much earlier, and the practical means to travel through real space came somewhat later.

Space was first conquered in 1923 in the pages of a slim book with the title of *The Rocket into Interplanetary Space.* It was written by a young mathematician named Hermann Oberth, who had to pay for part of the expense of getting it published. To most people, it was difficult, filled mostly with mathematics. Yet to people who could understand, it was the most exciting book ever published. It proved beyond all question that men could travel into space — and it showed how it could be done! Without ever having built a rocket at that time, Hermann Oberth had made a science of rocketry and had blazed the path to the depths of space!

It took time and immense amounts of work to turn the scientific knowledge into engineering fact, however. Eight years later, in 1931, the first liquid-fuel rocket was flown publicly; it was 2 feet high, weighed about 11 pounds, and rose to a height of less than 1,500 feet. It took 11 years more before the first V-2 proved for all time that a real load-carrying rocket could fly dependably.

Man first knocked at the door of space early in 1949 when a small WAC-Corporal rocket was lifted by a V-2. The blast of the smaller rocket carried it 250 miles up — into the beginnings of real space, where there is almost no air.

The "Birds," as the tiny satellites announced by the President were called, were sent up to almost the same height. But instead of falling back directly, they were placed in a circular orbit at a speed of 18,000 miles an hour, to keep circling around the Earth once each 90 minutes while the instruments inside the basketball-sized "Birds" sent back information on space by radio beams. However, they were not quite out in real space; there was still some air, and the tiny trace of friction from that gradually slowed the little satellites until they eventually fell back to Earth, burning up in the friction of the thicker air.

The real practical conquest of space began with the building of the first space station, about ten years after the first "Birds" went up. Oberth had already explained why such a station would be needed, and Wernher von Braun, Willy Ley and others had worked out how it could be done much earlier. But it was a huge job, requiring tremendous efforts and costing billions of dollars.

The building of this was covered in *Step to the Stars*. Jim Stanley had dreamed of going into space, but had almost given up hope. Then, suddenly, he was hired by a secret project and found he was to be one of the men who were to build the first station in space.

It wasn't an easy job. Up where there was no air except what could be brought up in tanks, where the circling of the station balanced out the pull of the Earth until there was no feeling of weight, and where everything was new and unusual, accidents were inevitable. Political troubles, sabotage, and unexpected difficulties all slowed down the work, until it seemed that the station might never be finished.

In the end, Jim was forced to take over the building of the station in a mock mutiny against the Major Electric Company, which was building the station. But the station was finished, and on time. Man's first foothold in space was now established. And most of the work of reaching the Moon and the planets had been done.

The big station was located at a distance of 1,075 miles from the Earth, circling the planet below once every two hours, exactly as the Moon circles each 28 days without falling. But while it was only the first thousand miles away against the 239,000 miles distance of the Moon, most of the work of getting to the Moon is done in those first thousand miles. The station traveled at a speed of 15,840 miles an hour, and a rocket had to develop about six miles a second speed to reach it!

To reach the Moon, however, a rocket needed only to add another mile or so a second to the speed of the station. It was almost impossible for any rocket men could build to take off from Earth, fly to the Moon, and return; it was just within the limits of possibility to reach the station. But a ship could be built at the station, fueled there, and then sent to the Moon without using fuels or techniques not known as early as 1950!

In space, the first thousand miles are harder than all the rest of the distance to even Mars or Venus!

And because he knew this, Jim Stanley wasn't too surprised when he learned that such a trip to the Moon was being planned. The cautious, scientific estimates of Wernher von Braun had indicated men should reach the Moon within ten years of the building of the space station. But science nearly always moves faster than the scientists dare to predict. The techniques learned in building the station had made it possible for the Moon trip to be made within another year — it simply required enough people who wanted to go badly enough.

Men had dreamed of the Moon for centuries. Lucian of Samosata wrote a book about travel to the Moon 1,800 years ago — but he was careful to warn the reader that it couldn't happen, and wasn't true! Less than a hundred years ago, men began to realize it could be done — maybe in another thousand years! Then Oberth proved it could be done this century. Men who had dreamed suddenly began to plan, and to fight to make those plans come true.

Those men weren't ready to wait any longer. And the men, like Jim Stanley, who helped to build the satellite station as the first steppingstone to space had no intention of stopping there.

This, then, is the account of how such men will make the trip. For the scientific facts, I am indebted to Wernher von Braun and Willy Ley, and to *Collier's* which published *Man on the Moon.* I have tried to make this an accurate picture of the trip they have outlined. But if there are errors, I hope someday they will be pointed out to me by one of the readers — one who will be writing the letter after his return from the first trip to the Moon!

L.D.R.

Chapter 1 - Return to Space

A THOUSAND miles beyond Hawaii, the big jet plane began to nose down for a landing at Johnston Island. Jim Stanley had been asleep in one of the two passenger seats, but now he awoke at the change in the speed. He sat up, yawning, and began buckling his seat belt, grinning self-consciously at the man in major's uniform who sat opposite him. Jim was a short, stocky young man, and the thin nylon shorts and shirt he wore emphasized his build, as well as showing the muscles that hard work had given him. Under the crew-cut, carroty-red hair, blue eyes looked out from a sprinkling of freckles around his snub nose.

The major smiled back, staring at the weight-saving uniform Jim wore. "First trip up to the space station?" he asked.

"Third," Jim corrected him. "I was part of the crew that built it."

The other man frowned in surprise, and then studied him more closely. The surprise on his face deepened as he stuck out a hand quickly. "You're Jim Stanley! No wonder I thought your face looked familiar. Wait'll I tell my boy I met the man who led the mutiny that finished the job up there!"

Jim started to deny it, but the plane was touching the water and there was no time for explanations. Besides, it would have done no good to refute the story the newspapers had built up around the finishing of Earth's first station a thousand miles out in space.

When Major Electric Company had fallen behind on the building of the station, they had sent out Jonas, their top troubleshooting executive. He'd needled the men into "mutiny" by pretending to stop the work. And when Jim had led the revolt to get the job finished, Jonas had stood by, secretly helping in every way he could. But the picture of a bunch of men fighting against the Company and nearly killing themselves to prove the job could be done in time had made too good a newspaper account to be altered by the facts.

It didn't matter. The important thing was that the station was up there now, circling the Earth every two hours. Man's first real step into space had been taken, and the next one — the long trip to the Moon-was now about to begin. At least Jim could think of no other reason for his being called back.

Johnston Island was busier than ever as Jim stepped off the plane. New buildings had been erected since he'd been there last, and he could barely see the tips of the great rocket ships over them. Then he heard his name called, and turned toward the man waiting for him in a jeep.

Mark Emmett waved, and slid over on the seat. "Hi, Jim! You look good." The small slim man was the ace rocket pilot for the ships that supplied the station, and the one who had first gotten Jim his job. Now he swung back to the wheel and began gunning the jeep toward the rocket field.

"No medical red tape this time, boy," he told Jim. "Colonel Halpern's yelling for you. Even had me hold up the takeoff, if I had to!"

Jim blinked at that. Rocket takeoffs had to be precisely timed. "Don't tell me they've built the Moon ships already?" he asked.

"Nothing that good," Mark answered. "It's Halpern's kid, Freddy. He stowed away on the ferry for the relay station. Hid in a box of supplies and wasn't found until the ferry was back. So you're supposed to rescue his precious little hide!"

"What happened to the regular ferry pilot?"

"Appendicitis, of all things. Dr. Perez was operating on him when they got word on Freddy. So they put in a rush call for you."

Jim sat back in sudden disgust at his former hopes.

He'd been almost sure that the Moon rockets must have been finished ahead of schedule, and that he was being called back for the piloting job he'd been promised. And now this! He couldn't share Mark's dislike of Halpern's somewhat spoiled, fifteen-year-old son, but he couldn't work up any enthusiasm for rescuing him from his foolishness now, either.

"What about the Moon ships?" he asked. There was still a chance that it was more than just Freddy's plight that was involved.

9

But Mark's shrug ended that hope. "Who knows?" he said. "You'll see soon enough. But don't get your hopes up too high."

He refused to say anything else. Jim was left with the conflicting rumors he had heard — rumors that ranged from the statement that the first trip to the Moon had already been made to speculation that the whole project had been called off. Maybe he'd been a fool to take off six months for boning up on theory at Central Tech. At least, if he had stayed on at the station as ferry pilot, he'd have known what was developing.

But he knew better. He'd won his pilot's license as a reward for his work on the station, but all his experience with the little space taxis that operated between rocket and station was still too little. He'd needed the cramming and education badly, if he was to prove adequate for the job of guiding one of the bigger Moon rockets!

They swung around a maze of buildings and onto the rocket field. Ahead, the big, three-stage rocket was waiting, rising over 260 feet from its finned base. Tankers were finishing fueling it with hydrazine, nitric acid and hydrogen peroxide. Mark glanced at his watch, braked to a screeching halt beside the rocket, and motioned for Jim to follow him toward the waiting elevator crane. The platform began to rise at once, lifting them up to the airlock near the top of the ship.

Lee Yeng and Hank Andrucci, copilot and radar-man, were already buckled into their seats in front of their screens, and the automatic pilot machines were humming over the course tapes. Jim fastened himself down, mentally bracing himself for the acceleration of takeoff. Then Mark reached for the starting button as the chronometer hand moved to the zero mark.

From below, there was the muffled thunder of the first stage blasting out. The ship seemed to shake and lift slowly. Then speed began building up, and the pressure of acceleration shoved Jim back into the seat. Now he seemed to weigh triple his normal poundage as the ship roared up and began to turn.

Abruptly, the pressure dropped as the first big stage broke away and started falling back toward the sea, now twenty-five miles below them. The second stage with its lighter load began blasting almost at once. Two minutes later, it also dropped away, leaving only the winged final stage that carried the men and freight to their destination. Its motor went on for another minute and a half, driving them to their maximum speed of eighteen thousand miles an hour.

When the final stage's motors cut off, they were coasting free, heading out into space. They would continue to slow as the Earth pulled back on them, but their momentum would carry them out to the station.

Jim breathed deeply in relief as the crushing pressure ended. With the ship coasting, there was no feeling of the gravity that was pulling back on the rocket and the men equally; gravity could be felt only when there was a resistance to keep whatever it acted on from being drawn toward the attracting mass. He waited, wondering if the long months had ruined his adaptation to lack of weight. There was a slight feeling of uneasiness for a second as his sense of balance tried to adjust. Then his sight took over the job that the feeling of up and down could no longer perform. He sighed again and relaxed. He could still take it. "How's it feel?" Mark asked.

Jim grinned back, stretching. "As if I'd inherited a million dollars," he said. He hadn't realized how much he'd grown to hate the constant pull of gravity on Earth. He'd grown up to take it for granted, until his first trip back from the station. But once free — or partially free, after the spin of the station gave it an apparent one-third gravity pull — it was hard to return to full weight. Here the body relaxed completely. It was like lying in a pool of buoyant water, without the temperature change or wetness.

The pumps began operating, changing the air in the rocket to match what they would find at the station. The pressure dropped slowly to three pounds as pure oxygen replaced the mixture of oxygen and helium. He heard Andrucci's voice, humming a current tune; he'd almost forgotten how the bass sounds thinned out in the lower pressure. Then his ears adjusted.

The gyroscopes began turning the ship around, getting it into position to match orbits with the station. Here, without air to aid in steering or hinder free motion, gyroscopic control was the simplest and cheapest. Every ounce of weight carried up counted for more than ten pounds of fuel at takeoff, so that even the men's hair was clipped before the trip, and the method requiring least weight was always the cheapest.

There was nothing to do while they drifted upward, with their speed dropping to less than fifteen thousand miles an hour. During the fifty minutes of free flight, the talk was mostly about unimportant things. Mark examined the tiny microfilms and reading device Jim was bringing with him to continue his studies, and nodded at the selection.

"You'll be ready enough for the big jump," he decided. "That is, if they ever make it."

"If?" Jim stared at him, feeling his doubts grow again. "I thought it was all settled."

"Is anything ever settled?" Mark asked. He grimaced. "After the mess of troubles you had with the station, you should know better. There are plenty of people who don't want the Moon trip — aren't even happy about the station."

There was certainly enough truth in that. In a few years the station would pay for itself in accurate weather predictions, as well as the scientific work being done, even without the value of its position as a base for military uses. But the first fire of enthusiasm had worn thin in a few months after it was finished. Now people seemed uncertain and worried, scared by the knowledge that guided missiles from the station could reach any place on Earth.

There were plenty of men who wanted to see man reach the Moon, too. But if it came to a test of which side held the power, Jim wasn't sure who would win.

He'd taken it for granted that it was settled. Jonas had told him that Major Electric had contracts to build the ships for the trip. It was naturally still a secret project, so there could be no news in the papers of any progress. He'd expected that the work would be going on while he studied. Now, apparently, Mark had nearly given up hope — and as one of the men who would bring up the materials, Mark should know as well as anyone.

They reached the top of their orbit, and Mark set the controls for the brief blast that would bring them up to the speed and orbit of the station. The rocket motors went on for fifteen seconds, and then they were drifting a quarter mile from the station.

It looked good to Jim. Shaped like a great metal-clad

doughnut, except for a hub and two spokes, it glistened in the sun as it swung around the immense globe of the Earth. The construction crew was gone, but the staff of eighty had taken over the quarters throughout its nearly eight hundred feet of circumference.

The little sausage-shaped space taxi Jim had piloted so long was already coming out to meet the rocket. It turned and drifted against the airlock, its silicone rubber front forming an airtight seal. Mark and Jim released the seals of their lock and stepped into the smaller ship.

Jim's old friend, Terry Rodriguez, was piloting the taxi, but Jim had barely time to nod to him and make a quick grab for his hand before an older man in military uniform was beside him. Colonel Halpern's face was both worried and relieved as he saw Jim.

"Sorry to yank you back," he began at once. "And thanks for coming. You're technically not under my command, but I knew I could count on you. How long before you can take off for the relay station?"

Jim shrugged, disregarding the apology. Major Electric and the Army had worked together well enough that no question of command was involved. "I slept on the plane, sir," he answered. "I can take off at once."

"Good!" The colonel sighed and finally managed a smile. "I wouldn't ask it if it were just that fool kid of mine. But the packing crate he hid in was supposed to contain material they need out there. Grab a cup of coffee in the commissary, and I'll have your orbit figured at once."

They settled against the entrance to the hub of the station, and the airlock hissed open quickly. Jim stepped out, breathing in the air that had grown sweeter to him than anything Earth could offer. He had the feeling of having come home from a long trip, and he realized again that anyone who had grown used to space could never feel completely at ease on any normal world again.

Then he gasped, and the sweetness of his homecoming was suddenly gone.

From a quartz window in the hub he could look back toward the pile of supplies for the Moon ships. There were no ships being built there. There wasn't even the beginning of the first framework.

13

In fact, as he studied it, he couldn't see that there was any increase in the amount of material there since he'd last seen it.

He couldn't believe it, but it looked as if men had given up the whole idea of going to the Moon!

Chapter 2 - Two Is a Crowd

THE RELAY station was being built a little over 22,000 miles above Earth's surface — the furthest men had yet gone in space. At that distance it would circle around the Earth once each twenty-four hours. And since Earth revolved in the same period of time, the same spot on the map would always be turned to face it.

The idea had been mentioned often, but not taken too seriously until the big station had been completed. Then the television and high frequency radio networks had realized how valuable it would be. Those frequencies had been limited to a little more than a hundred miles, since they traveled in straight lines, while the surface of the planet was curved. The networks had been forced to depend on many stations, spaced close together and linked by expensive cables and relays. But from a single station, such radio waves could be sent up through Earth's atmosphere to the station, which would beam them back — with the assurance that they would reach every section of the hemisphere. The energy for the rebroadcast would come from the sun, using solar batteries invented in the early fifties, and only a tiny crew would be needed. It meant a huge saving, particularly since the South American Republics were contributing for the use of channels in Spanish, and the United States was officially behind the plan as a help in official informational broadcasting. Unlike the original station or the planned trip to the Moon, everyone was in favor of this.

The relay station had been barely started when Jim left, but he'd made a few trips up as pilot of the ferry. The little ship was about four times the size of a taxi. There was a sphere in front for the pilot, and a bank of rocket motors behind. Between was mostly open space, with big nylon tanks for the fuel and a section of heavy netting to hold cargo. Up here, beyond the atmosphere, no streamlining was needed.

Nor did the little ship need heavy acceleration. Jim cut on the blast easily, building up speed gradually.

The big station rotated around Earth at a speed of 15,840 miles an hour, and he needed less than an additional mile a second to reach the relay station. As the ferry built up speed, he began pulling ahead of the main station and outward. After a few minutes, he cut off the blast. The ferry would continue on until it was time several hours later to match orbits at the top of its climb.

Below him, the Earth filled most of his field of view. It was an unusually clear day, apparently. Most of Africa could be recognized, though Europe was partly hazed over. Jim studied the planet for a few minutes, and then pulled out the viewer and began going over the engineering microfilms.

For a moment he wondered how Nora Prescott was doing with her studies at the Florida Rocket School. She had been a nurse on the station, but during the so-called mutiny she had become his assistant with the taxi, and had been offered a berth as his assistant pilot on the Moon ship. He had taken some courses in space piloting before coming to the station, but this was her first formal education on rockets. It must be a tough grind for her.

The ship drifted on, and he buried his nose in the viewer, until the timer warned him he was nearing apogee — the furthest distance from Earth.

He looked out of the dome of the ferry then. At twenty-two thousand miles up, space consisted almost entirely of nothing. In a billion cubic miles, there might have been a speck of dust or a pinhead-sized meteorite — though probably not — in addition to the few undetectable molecules in even such a vacuum as this. The stars were tiny hot points, too far away to consider. The Moon was still nearly the same. But Earth had shrunk. It was still forty times the apparent size of the Moon, but it no longer seemed to fill half the heavens.

Nothing else was visible on the screens. Then the radar spotted the relay station, and Jim brought it into view. He whistled. When he had seen it before, it had been a pile of junk and girders lying free in space. Now it was a sphere thirty feet across, with a huge net being built below it. This would be the antenna, and was the trickiest part of the construction.

His piloting had been better than he had expected. He opened the rocket motors carefully a few seconds, but matching course this time was easy. A minute later, he was within a few hundred feet of the relay station.

Before he was completely in his space suit he heard a thumping on the airlock. With a grin, he released the lock and stuck out a hand to help the two figures inside.

Through the plastic-faced helmets, he could see the grinning faces of his former foreman, Dan Bailey, and the project engineer, Thorndyke.

"Forget your cargo," Thomdyke's voice sounded in his earphones. "I've got men coming out to unload you. Come on over for a chance to talk."

Jim nodded, more than willing. The two men jumped out into space, and Jim followed. Once such a feat had seemed almost miraculous to him, but now he was used to it. He sighted on the relay station lock and kicked off, almost without thinking, to drift after them until his momentum carried him the few hundred feet and he could reach the handholds.

Inside, the completed sphere was packed with sleeping bags, but Bailey led the way through them, shucking off his suit as he went. He pointed to the confusion, grinning. "Not like the big station, lad. Getting a hundred men in here is a bit crowded. But we're managing. Lack of gravity helps, now that we're all used to it. Here, let me have a look at you."

They made their way to the tiny section of nylon sheets that served as an office, where Dan's wife already had plastic bottles of coffee waiting for them. "Sit down, boy," Dan said. "It's good to see you again."

"Good to be back," Jim told him. And then somehow there was nothing to say. He could see their progress, and there didn't seem to be anything about his schooling worth mentioning. He watched the others silently for a moment, before realizing that something was wrong. They had the same vaguely worried look he'd seen in his brief stay at the main station.

But it was Thorndyke who brought it up. "Notice anything odd on your way up, Jim?" he asked.

Jim shook his head. "Such as?"

The engineer shrugged, and Dan fidgeted with his coffee before answering. Then the foreman blurted it out. "Another relay station being built, maybe!"

"We've spotted something," Thorndyke amplified quickly. "We have a small scope here — big enough to see the station. Lately we've seen something going on. We can't see details, but when the station's over the South Pole, we see a bright spot at the same height over the North Pole. We sent down a note to Halpern, but got nothing but silence from him. Any rumors down below?"

Jim shook his head again. "Nothing like that. But why should we build another station?" Then he stopped, staring at them. "You mean the Combine's trying it?"

Dan shrugged doubtfully. "We don't know, Jim. But who else?"

The Combine was the big union of European and Asiatic nations which had given some of the trouble with the building of the station. Combine scientists had even managed to get an atomic-powered rocket up briefly before it exploded. Jim and Mark Emmett had rescued the men on it, and after that the hostility had seemed to fade somewhat. But lately, debating at the World Congress indicated it was picking up again. It was mostly because of potential danger from the Combine that the United States was forced to use the station as a military base.

"But I thought we proved they couldn't do it," Jim protested. "When we picked up their wrecked men, we showed that we could protect ourselves. No other orbit would be safe from ours. Mr. Thorndyke, they wouldn't dare risk building another station. And we couldn't let them."

With two stations, things would be worse than ever. True, their own station could reach any part of the Earth with missiles before a war could get a full start. But if the Combine had its own station up there, war couldn't be prevented; striking at the danger on Earth would do no good if the Combine station could then send its missiles against the United States.

"Sure. Sure, I guess you're right," Thorndyke agreed slowly. But Jim could see he wasn't convinced. "Up here, one is company and two's a crowd we couldn't permit. All the same, there's something there!"

Then he glanced at the clock and jumped up, catching a handhold to prevent overshooting. "Hey, it's almost time for departure, and you haven't picked up your passenger. I've got the kid strapped into a sleeping bag. I wouldn't mind his being up here, but I figure I'd better make his stay unpleasant enough that he won't try tricks again. Want to take over now?"

They moved through the crowded sphere again, putting on their suits. Jim could see that most of the work here was finished, and that the relay station was almost ready to operate. Dan Bailey saw his glances and read them correctly. "Almost done," he admitted, and there was more worry on his face. "Dunno what we do then. We were counting on working on the Moon ships, but. . . Oh, well, I suppose we can learn to live on Earth again, if we have to."

Thorndyke threw a warning glance at Dan, but Jim had heard enough to know that the men here had also given up hopes of any immediate trip to the Moon. And he remembered that he was in the same fix for the future. He was being carried on Major Electric's books under its contract to build ships for the trip to the Moon. If that were canceled . . .

They found Freddy Halpern then. The boy was a slightly built, thin-featured kid who looked two years younger than his age. He scowled at Thorndyke, and then spotted Jim. "You taking me back to Dad?" he asked.

Jim nodded. "That's orders."

"Good. I'm sick of being tied up here!" Then the boy grinned. "I showed them, though, didn't I? Dad wouldn't let me go, but I got here!"

"Yeah," Jim admitted. "You got here — and almost cost your father his command."

Yet he still couldn't dislike Freddy. The motherless boy had been brought to the main station, where he was surrounded by busy scientists and military men, too excited over their work to bother with a youngster. He'd been spoiled by a grandmother on Earth, but there wasn't anything mean about him. And while he often talked and acted younger than his age, Jim knew there was nothing wrong with his intelligence.

"Forget it," he told the boy. "Get into your suit and let's get going."

There was no protest. Dan helped them on with their helmets. "I suppose you'll be piloting the ferry regularly, Jim, so we'll be seeing you," he said. "Maybe next trip we can really talk."

Then Jim and Freddy were kicking off into space, and back to the ferry. It hadn't been the happy reunion Jim had pictured. But then, nothing was working out as he'd pictured it!

Inside the ferry and out of their suits, Freddy made a beeline for the controls. His voice broke with excitement. "Jim, can I pilot going back? I've been using the taxi some — Terry lets me handle it. I'll be careful, if you'll let me try!"

"Not this trip," Jim told him, pulling him back and half forcing him into the other seat. Then, at the boy's expression, he relented a little. He'd had his own experiences at being alone with busy adults when his father had been a construction engineer. "Tell you what, Freddy. I've got some microfilms here. You study them first to learn how it's done, and then maybe I'll let you try some other trip."

The boy nodded quickly, his fingers trembling as he took the viewer and the film Jim had selected. He made no further move toward the controls as Jim blasted off, cutting speed so that they would begin falling back toward the big station.

It was an hour later when the boy whistled, and Jim looked over his shoulder at the little screen. Freddy had found a film that covered the theory of flight to the Moon, together with one of the standard orbits.

For a minute, Jim considered asking Freddy about the trip. It was obviously something that was of paramount interest to the boy. Then he shrugged. Even if Freddy knew, it wasn't his place to pry out information Halpern and the authorities weren't ready to give.

With nothing else to do, he sat staring through the control bubble while Freddy read on. The Earth was growing steadily, and now Jim could just make out the reflection of the station. In a little more than an hour they'd be back — back from the farthest in space that men had gotten, and what seemed to be the farthest they would ever go. He tried to adjust his thinking to the delay on the big jump.

He knew that the original plans of Dr. von Braun on which this was still based had put the Moon trip ten years after the building of the station. But with new structural materials and what they had learned of space, it didn't have to wait now!

Then a flash of light from the Earth below caught Jim's eye. Apparently, seeing must have been excellent on the part of the night side below him. The light rose upward, a tiny speck on the huge area, but clear enough to trace. It could only be the blast of a big first stage.

Then he groaned as realization hit him. No rocket should be taking off from that section! And hasty figuring of its orbit showed that it couldn't be headed for the station — but that it could very well be aimed at a spot 180° behind, which was the ideal spot for any attempt at building a Combine station!

Bailey and Thorndyke must have been right! There was another station going up, where two wasn't just a crowd, but a threat to the whole world!

Chapter 3 - Rocket Trail

HALPERN was waiting in the taxi when Jim matched orbit with the station. Halpern took one look at his son and pulled the boy to the back of the taxi. Jim couldn't hear what was said, but he saw Freddy's face whiten. When they got out in the hub of the station, Dr. Perez was waiting to take the boy in tow for a medical checkup.

Halpern sighed as they left and motioned Jim to follow him toward the simple office where he held command. It was near the outer section of the station, where the spin gave a comfortable but low imitation of gravity. "Any trouble with the boy?" he asked Jim.

"Not with the boy," Jim answered. "Maybe you should let him train for piloting."

"I probably will, someday. If he's able to take it." The older man sighed again, staring down at his desk. "I wish I had more time for him. This isn't the best place to bring him up, I guess. But it's no good for him down there, either . . . Umm, wait a minute. You said you didn't have trouble with *him.* Does that mean you had trouble with something else?"

Jim had thought the colonel had missed his remark, but he was relieved at the opening it gave him. He told briefly what he had heard at the relay station and what he'd seen on the way back. Halpern had frowned slightly at first, but now he sat listening with a woodenly official lack of expression, making no comments until Jim had finished.

His voice was carefully unexcited as he acknowledged the report. "I'll add it to our next message back, of course. And I appreciate your reporting it directly to me. Now I'll have to ask you not to discuss it with anyone else. With our relations with the Combine still somewhat strained, we can't have idle rumors going around. And . . ."

"That rocket trail wasn't idle rumor," Jim interrupted him hotly.

The colonel nodded. "No, I didn't mean that. I assume you

can recognize it accurately. But that doesn't mean anyone is trying to build another station. The Combine was experimenting with rocket ships before they tried that atomic-powered model, and they're probably working on liquid fuels again. That's normal enough. And at this distance you'll have to admit that you can't trace an orbit too well. You have no way of knowing it was making a trip to this height. Or have you?"

"No, sir," Jim admitted. But he wasn't convinced, and he had the feeling that Halpern was no more convinced than he was. He'd run into the seemingly logical official method of covering up before. Obviously, Halpern had already known something was going on. Then he switched over to his other worry. "When do they really start work on the Moon ships, Colonel Halpern?"

The older man sighed heavily. "You know as much as I do, Jim. It's supposed to be in civilian hands now."

Terry Rodriguez was waiting as Jim came out of the colonel's office. The little man had stayed on at the station as head of the maintenance crew, as well as taking over the handling of the taxi. He never had much to say, and Jim was grateful for the fact as they headed toward the commissary to eat. After the first few words of general conversation, they ate in silence.

Terry stood up first. "I've got to inspect something over at the doghouse," he said. The doghouse was the separate little bubble that housed the astronomical telescope and was following the station at a short distance. "If you want to sack in, you've got the same quarters, Jim. See you tomorrow?"

Jim nodded and watched him leave. He stared about at the others eating, realizing that he hardly knew anyone here now. The scientists and military men had replaced the old construction crew, and he was practically a stranger here.

Finally, he headed for the cubicle that was his home aboard. He dropped gratefully onto the elastic hammock that served as a bed. After the relaxation possible here, no bed could ever feel completely comfortable in the heavier gravity of Earth. He'd looked forward to a chance to sleep here again. But now his thoughts were too busy to let him take advantage of the opportunity.

He'd been basing his whole thoughts of the future on the

Moon trip. Without it, he had no real business in space. The pilots up from Earth had to be topnotch aviation men first, to handle the landing through the atmosphere, and Jim had only the school training in that. He had no scientific or military use. Of course, he might hang on to ferry supplies to the relay station for a while, but once it was finished, only occasional trips would be needed, and those could be handled by one of the regular pilots. The only place left would be back on Earth. Jonas would probably be willing to place him somewhere in Major Electric, and he had money enough from the fabulous salary of a spaceman to carry him. But he'd grown used to this type of life, and he didn't intend to be grounded unless nothing else was left! Besides, if the Combine were building a station, in spite of Halpern's careful doubts, Earth wouldn't be too pleasant a place for anyone to live!

Jim finally drifted off to sleep, still bothered by the thoughts. He was in the middle of some vague nightmare of being tied up and unable to move when a hand on his shoulder awakened him. Even before he opened his eyes, he knew it was well before the time when he would normally have wakened.

It was Halpern, and the colonel reached forward to shake his shoulder again. Then he saw that Jim was awake, and dropped down on the edge of the hammock. "Emergency, Jim," he said bitterly. "We seem to have a jinx, or something. Gantry and his copilot ran into trouble. A new passenger up went crazy when weight cut off, and they had quite a fracas before they could subdue him. The copilot's got a concussion, and Gantry wants you to replace him."

Jim realized that Halpern was putting it as a request, rather than an order. It was indicated by the fact that the colonel had come himself, instead of sending an aide. But there was no question about his going. A chance to serve as copilot on the big ships was more than he'd been able to hope for; he'd had one brief try at it when they had rescued the Combine men, but that had been a special case.

He was off the hammock and getting into his thin suit at once. Then he stopped, puzzled. "How come Gantry doesn't just wait until another copilot can be shipped up?"

"He would, if he had to. But we've got a special shipment going back. More of the cancer serum. The first tests looked so good that Earth's screaming for more — and with all the trouble we've been having, we need all the good will and publicity we can get."

It was reason enough. Up here where a whole laboratory could be evacuated to a nearly perfect vacuum at any desired low temperature, chemical reactions were possible that couldn't be done on Earth. It only took a few ounces of hormones or such serums as this for thousands of treatments. Jim had known they were working on something to cure cancer, but he hadn't realized there'd been any real progress yet.

Halpern turned to leave. He looked tired — more so than Jim had seen him before — but he managed to smile. "Thanks again, Jim. And better rush it. Take-off's pretty near."

Jim found Terry waiting with the taxi, and there was a hasty breakfast set up for him to eat while they moved out. Gantry was ready with the lock by the time they reached the rocket.

Jim followed the big man back to the controls. He'd never gotten to know the pilot well — even Gantry's own copilot didn't seem too close to him. He was the exact opposite of most of the pilots. He was a big, heavily built man in a job where low weight was of the utmost importance; where the preference was given to young men, he was over forty. And there was nothing devil-may-care about him. He had been forced to fight for whatever he achieved, and he had lost all sense of fun, apparently. He'd made up his mind as a boy that he'd pilot the first rocket. Time had run out on him, but he hadn't quit. He must have been rejected a hundred times — but he'd made it.

Jim headed for the copilot's seat, stepping aside to let Gantry take the pilot's position. But the man shook his head. "You have it backward, Stanley," he said evenly. "You're the pilot this trip. I sprained my wrist in the mixup." He dropped to the copilot's seat, passing over the course charts. "We're awaiting your orders, sir!" For a second, the universe seemed to reel under Jim. He had a pilot's license, of course, but — He was sure Halpern hadn't known. No sane man would assign him to such a job. An atmospheric landing! Yet Gantry was sane, and he had made the decision.

Then Jim caught himself and began buckling himself down while he went over the calculations Gantry had prepared. "Thank you, Mr. Gantry," he said.

Surprisingly, the big man smiled. "I'm named Ed, Jim. Glad to have you aboard." And then, as if explaining everything, he waved toward the station. "It took a man who knew what he wanted and how to do it to build that."

Coming from Gantry, this was probably the highest type of compliment. But Jim had no time to appreciate it. The chronometer was nearing zero. He began calling the orders, as he'd heard Mark call them before. The hand of the chronometer moved on steadily. Then it hit the mark.

Mercifully, the controls were the same as those on the ferry. Jim's hands moved out steadily to them, while the big automatic pilot went into operation. It had been designed to do a better job than men could do, but men had been designed to do the impossible. With enough experience, the pilots had found that they could shade the controls just enough to make up for variations in the blast before the automatic pilot was aware of them. Under Gantry's eyes, Jim hesitated, then began juggling the verniers. He'd managed the trick on his other flight, and it felt right this time.

Gantry nodded when the blast cut off. "Very good, Jim. We'll leave it at that."

The rocket began drifting back and down toward Earth. For fifty minutes, there was nothing more to be done. This time there wouldn't be even a turnover, since they'd hit the air nose first, to coast through the thin atmosphere on their wings and controls, using the friction as a brake to halt their speed.

Jim was frantically digging through his mind for everything he could remember on such a maneuver. He'd had some practice in rocket-propelled high altitude planes at the school, and he'd seen Mark make the run. He also knew the theory. But by the time they hit, it would have to be done almost automatically, which meant he had to be ready with the answers beforehand.

His hands were sweating slightly. It occurred to him that he could probably depend on Gantry in any real emergency; a sprained wrist was bad, but it could be used. Still, it was his responsibility now. He glanced back at the radarman and saw worry on the man's face. Then Gantry's eyes met his, and his look steadied him. If

Gantry had any doubts, he wasn't showing them. He'd decided it all back at the station, and was sticking by the decision.

Earth's pull was acting on them now, building their speed up to more than five miles a second. It would be enough to burn them to a cinder — as the original tiny satellites had burned on striking the air. The upper fringes of the atmosphere were drawing near. Jim began to brace himself.

Abruptly Gantry grunted and pointed to the screen. "Combine rocket again," he said.

There was a long rocket trail rising below them. At this distance, there could be no mistake. It was tilting from its vertical rise into the regular synergy curve of a ship heading out to an orbit. From Gantry's expression, it was a fairly familiar sight.

There was no question now. The Combine was in space, and Halpern must have known it.

Then the controls in Jim's hands began to show evidence that they were touching atmosphere.

Chapter 4 - Half a Billion Dollars

THE DESCENT through the atmosphere was the longest and hardest job for any of the rocket pilots, and they were at the beginning of the tough part now. The rocket was halfway around the world from where it had left the station, and fifty miles above the surface of Earth. Up there, the air was still incredibly thin, but at their speed, its friction had already begun to heat the hull.

The trick was to find the right density of air to cut their speed. If they were going too deep, the friction would heat them beyond the point where even the tough skin of the ship could stand it. If they weren't deep enough, they would lose speed too slowly and might land somewhere in midocean.

Jim kept his eyes on the pyrometers that showed the hull temperature, and on the chronometer. When he had a chance, he glanced at the other instruments, but the course was largely determined by time and temperature.

The needles rose rapidly. They passed the thousand-degree mark and went on. But they were supposed to do that. At the critical point, the hull would be thirteen hundred degrees hot! The ship had been designed for that, and there were machines that cooled the inside, though they had to count on the insulation for the biggest job.

Delicately, Jim maneuvered the stick that controlled their height. Inside, the temperature crept up slightly, but it felt even hotter than it was. He was remembering again the first tiny satellites men had sent out. At a much lower speed, they had finally dived back into the atmosphere and the friction of their fall had burned them to dust long before they struck the Earth.

Here the automatic pilot was nearly useless. Gantry's eyes were riveted on him, Jim saw in a quick glance. "Too deep?" he asked harshly of the pilot.

Gantry cleared his throat. "A touch, maybe. But you've got a little margin."

It helped to be reassured of that. He'd almost forgotten that it wasn't something that took absolute perfection. Now he suddenly relaxed, and it began to come easier.

They were speeding around the Earth at less than three miles a second now, and at a height of about thirty-five miles. The hull was still at red heat, but half the descent was over.

Once they reached the speed of two miles a second it became easier. Now the temperature began to fall slowly, and they were dropping in a long flat glide that should take them to the field.

From then on, the speed fell quickly, along with the temperature. They were soon at the normal cruising speed of a jet plane. Here Jim found himself the master of the ship. And then, curiously, as the speed fell, it grew harder again. He was tensing up because of the landing to be made.

But that proved easier than he had expected. As the field came into view, the radarman was in contact with the ground, and there was no question of needing a clear lane. There was always a clear lane provided for one of the returning rockets. The big ship came down easily, more slowly than the jet jobs Jim had been forced to land before. Its gliding speed was less than seventy miles an hour.

He felt the wheels touch, finally, and they were rolling down the long runway. He caught his breath and let it out in a deep sigh. He'd made it! Then they stopped, and Gantry was holding out the logbook for him to sign.

The big man looked as if he'd been under strain, too, but he shrugged casually. "The first times are the hard ones. Now you can take your pilot's license out of the mothballs and hang it on the wall!"

Out on the field Jim found a jeep waiting for him. Gantry would supervise the handling of the ship now, since no regular pilot would trust anyone else to do that. Jim's job was done, and he could give his nerves a chance to relax in a hotel room until the next takeoff took him back to the station.

Abruptly, he noticed that they weren't near the hotel, and turned to the driver. "Hey, I want the Haute Terre!"

"Sorry," the driver said, "Thought you knew. I've got orders to take you to see Mr. Jonas!"

Jim shrugged. He might have known. It had been a long time

29

since he'd seen the man, and some report was probably due. Then he frowned, as he considered it. After a trip like this, even Jonas should be willing to wait while he changed into normal Earth clothes and cleaned up. If something else had gone wrong . . .

He knew it had when he was first ushered into the man's local office. Jonas was still the perfect picture of an executive at a businessman's club, but there were deeper lines etched into his face, and his hair seemed even grayer. The voice was the same hearty one, though, as he grabbed Jim's hand.

"Hi, Jim. I heard you got your baptism under fire and did a fine job of it. Sorry I can't let you get the rest you deserve."

"What's up?" Jim asked.

Jonas dropped to a seat, indicating a chair for Jim. "You're not supposed to, but I expect you know about the Combine rockets we've spotted?" He waited for Jim's nod, and then went on. "Well, it's no secret any more! I've got an advance tipoff that the Combine has announced the whole thing. They're putting up a station on the other side of the Earth from our orbit location. And it couldn't have come at a worse time. I've been negotiating for the appropriation — lobbying, you might call it. It's being studied in a House Committee, but I was hoping to get it out with a recommendation this week. And now this news!"

"I thought your appropriation had gone through," Jim objected.

"The preliminary one and the contract, yes," Jonas said. He grimaced. "But on a government contract, things aren't that simple. They can still cancel, or refuse to allot the money. And for the Moon trip, we still need half a billion dollars. We can't gamble on starting without it!"

It was only an eighth of what the station had cost, or a quarter of the research on the atomic bomb. But it was still a huge figure. No private firm could provide it.

"But I don't see how that will be affected by news of the Combine station," Jim objected. "It means that we'll have to get to the Moon! Maybe they can build another station — I thought we'd proved that they couldn't — but they can't build another moon!"

Jonas sighed heavily. "Hindsight is better than nothing, Jim.

We know now that they can build a station, and we can't stop them. Sure, we could reach their platform with our missiles, as you proved before. We could drive them out of the skies, in theory. Then what? Would you sign an order to attack them?" The idea penetrated slowly. And then it was obvious to Jim, and he could have kicked himself for not seeing it before. So long as the Combine claimed their station was for scientific study, there was no excuse to stop them. They weren't overtly attacking, but anything that might be done to wreck their station would be considered an act of murder and war! If anything were done against them, the United States would be branded as an aggressor — by most of the world.

Until the Combine used their station for warlike purposes, nothing could be done against them. And once they did use it for such purposes, it would be too late.

"We could force it down, physically," Jonas explained. "But morally and politically, we can't. And that's going to make the resentment against our station flare up again. People are going to believe we started it all with the first one. It's like the atom bomb — people were so scared that they would have dropped the whole thing if they could. And in that kind of atmosphere you can't expect to get funds out of Congress. When the voters hate everything about space, what can their representatives do?"

"But if we get to the Moon — " Jim started to repeat.

Jonas shook his head. "The Moon is 239,000 miles away. Try to make people see that it can protect us when a station a thousand miles up cannot. They were sold on the space station as a way to end war. Now they will see it as the most dangerous possible weapon. They'll want no part of space!"

He stared at Jim bitterly. Then he settled back into the chair to gaze out of the window toward the rocket field. "Maybe we picked the wrong job, Jim. I could have stuck to our regular industrial divisions. You could probably have done all right as a mechanic. Maybe we were fools."

"As long as we got the station up, I won't think so, sir," Jim told him.

Jonas snorted. "Suppose it doesn't stay up? Having two stations sounds bad — but think about having none. And it's

31

possible. In a week there's going to be a yell going up to outlaw all stations and tear them down! Maybe if we'd had time enough to prove our station's value, like the weather study and that cancer serum work, we could win out. But now I don't know. There's always talk about outlawing anything which can be dangerous, and with people scared enough, maybe they could put over the idea this time."

For a while, the two men sat in silence, staring at each other. Jim was turning over Jonas' words, and he couldn't find a flaw in their logic. The station could be a dangerous weapon — and with two stations the tensions could increase until the danger was realized. He'd never even considered the possibility before that men might retreat from space permanently, and he didn't find it easy to take now.

Finally he stirred unhappily. "What's all this got to do with me, Mr. Jonas? You must have some angle, or you wouldn't have sent for me."

"It wasn't my idea," Jonas said. "Look, let me give you a little background. There are three key men on the Appropriations Committee. One of them wants to see us make the trip. One is dead set against it, but he'll go along with the majority in a vote on it — because he doesn't want to be known as an enemy of progress. The third hasn't made up his mind. Our only hope is to win him over. And he wants to talk to you."

"I can't tell him anything he couldn't learn from you," Jim pointed out. He knew his name had been in the newspapers often enough for everyone to realize he was completely convinced of the need of space travel. It hardly made him a neutral witness.

"I don't know why he wants you, though I can guess," Jonas said. "There are still some ugly rumors being kicked around about the fact that the Combine chief named his twins after you and Mark Emmett."

"You mean Peter Chiam? He's only the nephew of the leader over there!"

Jonas laughed harshly. "You mean he was! Now he's the leader. I told you we had a jinx. He succeeded his uncle two days ago, just before the Combine decided to announce this. The whole timing on it is sour."

It couldn't have been worse, Jim realized. When he and Mark had rescued Chiam from the Combine's unsuccessful atomic rocket, the man had named his children for them, probably as a gesture of gratitude. But a few papers had painted a dark picture of it, and some of the rumors might still be kicking around. If so, some people might even think there had been some connection with the Combine's getting its foothold in space.

It made no sense to Jim, but he'd heard enough of the results of rumor before to know what could happen.

"When are they coming?" he asked.

"They're flying out now. They won't trust this on the cable, so I've assigned our fastest jet plane to them. You've got plenty of time, and I'll notify you, but I wanted you to get used to the idea first." He sighed again. "I'm sorry about this, Jim. But we've got to prove our security regulations are tight, and they won't accept this fact without seeing you personally."

Jim couldn't see that his discretion would make the station any more or less valuable, or that the visit would prove anything the FBI hadn't already discovered in clearing him. But if Jonas thought he could help, he was willing to try.

Somehow, though, the prospect made him more nervous than the idea of landing the rocket had done. At least he'd known what to expect then. Now he couldn't even guess. And he didn't like the idea that any mistake he might make would perhaps determine the fate of all future space travel.

He found the jeep still waiting for him, and this time the driver started for the hotel without prompting. He had barely stepped into the lobby when Nora Prescott was rushing toward him, half laughing, half crying. After a moment she drew back to stare at him, and he had some staring of his own to do. It was the first time he'd ever seen her in Earth costume. And the long hair seemed strange on her, after the universal crew cut needed in space. She looked less thin, and even better than he remembered.

"They told me you were with Jonas," she was saying. "And I knew you'd be here eventually. I didn't even know you were down here until my plane landed! Why didn't you radio me?"

"I didn't know myself until I was ordered down," he told her. "And what about you? Why didn't you send up word?"

She laughed. "I guess that makes us even. But I just couldn't stop to think. The minute I finished schooling, I grabbed the first plane I could get. I couldn't wait to get back to the station."

Then she was fishing in her handbag and dragging out an official piece of paper that certified she had completed such and such courses of study and was ready for all types of work on rockets for use beyond the atmosphere.

He tried to sound sincere as he congratulated her, but he couldn't help wondering whether she'd ever have a chance to make use of it.

Chapter 5 - Dark Outlook

NORA had to leave for the long medical examination before her return to space. She had escaped some of it the first time, since there had been a desperate need for nurses then. But now she had to make up for it. Jim felt sorry for her, remembering his own experience. But he'd have been happy to exchange examinations with her.

The plane carrying the committee members arrived late in the afternoon, but Jonas called him to tell him that he wouldn't be quizzed until the next morning. As it turned out, Jim's examination was only one of a long list of inspections they were making on the Island project. "I can't say I'm surprised," the executive said. "They put so much emphasis on seeing you while you were down that they probably thought I'd figure on their taking the rest for granted. Anyhow, it gives you the rest of the day."

From his hotel window Jim could see Jonas' big car going by with the three men. They hardly looked like ogres. One white-haired man could have posed for Santa Claus with the help of a beard.

The evening papers carried the account of the Combine announcement. Jim found his way to the crowd that surrounded the newsstand in the lobby, and went back with a paper. There was little in it that Jonas hadn't told him, except that the station was to be a bigger, greatly improved model — "ending the monopolistic stranglehold now being held on the peaceful exploitation of mankind's frontiers in space," according to the official Combine release.

Jim had just finished lunch when the car called for him to take him to the meeting room in Jonas' office building. The white-haired man turned out to be Congressman Blounce. His handshake was friendly, and the other two were pleasant enough during the introductions. Their first questions seemed like those that anyone might ask of a man who had been in space.

There was no time when Jim could find any discourtesy. But

as the time wore on, the questions sharpened. Jim found soon enough that Jonas had been partly right and partly wrong. The chief interest was on Peter Chiam and the Combine atomic rocket — but apparently not because they suspected Jim of anything; their suspicions were that the Combine men might have seen too much.

The trouble was that the three men wanted to know more than Jim could tell them. He had seen Chiam once, for a short trip back from the disaster, and the man had been unconscious during most of that. In fact, he had said nothing beyond his first words of relief when they pulled him out. And there had been no chance for the investigating of the Combine rocket, since its driving mechanism had been ruined.

The committee members showed some interest in the troubles of the early days on the station, but they kept coming back to the business with Chiam. From a remark dropped by Blounce, who did most of the questioning, Jim gathered that they were going to interview Mark Emmett on the same things.

There was no question raised of Jim's patriotism, though they did ask a little about his revolt against authority during the so-called mutiny. Then, far sooner than he had expected from the way it had been going, they were thanking him and letting him go.

Jonas walked out with him. It was a cool day, but the man was sweating. Jim stared at him in surprise. "Blounce didn't seem too set against the big jump," he observed.

"Blounce is the one in favor of the ships," Jonas told him. "He was doing the questioning to keep it in the safest channels! What did you think of the others?"

"They didn't seem too interested," Jim answered.

Jonas grunted unhappily. "You're right. They seem to have made up their minds already, and this is just routine to them. I always suspect short investigations."

"You mean they've decided against us?"

"Maybe." Jonas stopped, about to return to the building. Then he shrugged. "Probably, Jim. I don't know. But you might do some praying on it. There's still one chance, and we'll have to hope for that."

Jim found from Personnel Service that he was slated to return to the station, but not for three more days, when Nora would be returning with him. He inquired for her, but found she was still in Medical. It left him with nothing to do but return to the hotel, and he walked the distance, watching the people. There was a general feeling of gloom everywhere, and he saw more than one person glance up at the skies with the shadow of fear on his face.

In his room, Jim found the maid cleaning. She studied him with doubtful, frightened eyes as she finished. At the door, she hesitated, pointing to the headline on the paper. "You going back to that station, sir?"

"As soon as I can," he answered. "Why?"

She shook her head. "You wouldn't catch me up there, not with that Combine thing now. Sometimes I think my dad was right. God never meant men going out there. Man just wasn't meant to leave this world until he dies."

Jim gasped, surprised. He'd seen letters filled with the "Man Wasn't Meant" theme in some of the papers, but he'd never expected to run across it here, in the center of the rocket development where even bus-boys knew all about space. He tried to smile. "If man had been meant to eat cooked food, he'd have been designed with a stove in his throat to cook it on the way down!"

The maid didn't smile back. She only frowned and went off down the hall with her equipment, shaking her head.

The next day Jim avoided people. It was obvious that Jonas had been right. Fear was turning to resentment, except on the part of those directly connected with space. But sitting alone in his room gave Jim the heebie-jeebies. He finally was relieved when he got a call from Cummings, one of the head engineers at the planning section of Major Electric.

"Jonas suggested I call you," Cummings said when he picked Jim up. "He remembers some of the trouble we ran into with the station, and he thought it might be a good idea for you to look over some of our plans. If you can read specs and blueprints, I'd like to know what a member of the construction crew thinks of the plans."

The building was a combined factory for specialized parts and engineering and drafting plant. Jim was amazed to find that there was almost no automatic work being done. In the small quantities they used, Cummings explained, it was cheaper to handform parts than to order automatic dies that might have to be changed at any time. "If we ever get space travel on mass production, the cost will come down to a tenth of what it is," he said. "But that's in the future, if it ever comes."

There were templates and tools being developed for the Moon ships, but no real work had been done yet. Jim lost interest in the manufacturing. Cummings took him through another huge room where the ordering of supplies was done, and into the drafting section.

There, progress had been made. The plans were almost finished, and Jim could find little wrong with them. "You're still making things to too tight a tolerance," he suggested at last. "Down here, milling to a thousandth of an inch is good design. But in space, where the sun's heat, and the cold in the shadows, twists and distorts things, it's better if you design for a lot of free play. Like this."

Cummings went through the plans with him, making notes where they applied. "Fine, we'll put these ideas through a calculating machine and it'll get the pattern, so we can catch anything else. How does it look?"

"Like a lot of paper work," Jim answered. He meant it as a joke, but his eyes went automatically to one of the big files where correspondence was stored.

Cummings laughed. "And you figure it's a waste of money we need, I suppose. Most people do. Here!" He pulled out a folder at random, and dug out a sheaf of papers after a quick look. "We need shock mounts on the landing legs of the ships. Light, strong, unaffected by cold or heat. We've been querying for suggestions, and we think we've finally found the answer — from a company which normally makes shock absorbers for fancy baby carriages! These cables and letters cost a lot of money, Jim — but if we'd had to start research to design our own shock mounts, it would have cost ten times as much. The paper work actually saves us money, in the long run."

It made sense. It didn't fit with the stories Jim had read about secret rockets being built in small plants to explore the stars, but he hadn't really believed them anyhow. It seemed that half the industrial firms of North America had folders here. Maybe the reason the United States had developed the station first was simply that she had more industries. It was a new idea to him, but he could find nothing wrong with it.

When he got back to his room with the latest papers, he found that the World Congress was holding a special meeting over the problem of the stations. The accounts of the first day didn't look good. The United States had protested the invasion of the first station's orbit, and the Combine had replied with a speech about monopoly and the dangers of having any single nation hold such power. From the news story, it was obvious that even many of the nations in the Alliance had been swayed. Fear of too much power in any hands was stirring, and there seemed many ready to believe there might be more safety in numbers. And already the suggestion of disarming all space stations and abandoning them had been made!

Most of the paper was devoted to that. But buried back in the inside, Jim found two other stories. One was an account of work at the station, in which he learned that scientists had been able to find the secret of cell division. The use of giant amoebas, nearly the size of baseballs, had given them the key to the problem. In Earth's gravity such single cells were impossible, but they were easy to grow in the weightless hub of the station. The second story was a preliminary report on the cancer serum, indicating it was already better than anything else ever used.

Someday, perhaps, as a result of work at the station, medical science would learn to cure all cancer and to make the cells divide to regrow amputated parts of the body. But the useful functions of the station were now nearly forgotten in the fears that had grown up.

Nora came out the nest day, looking a little shaken, but smiling happily as she displayed her medical certificate. She'd passed, indicating that her body had not suffered from the long months in space. Then she sobered as she caught up with the developments that had been going on.

"It looks bad," she admitted, but she refused to be completely miserable. "It looked bad before, Jim — and we found a way. We'll find it again. I heard Jonas say once that President Andrews is determined on getting us to the Moon, and he's a pretty resourceful man. What's playing at the movies?"

Jim hadn't looked before, too wrapped in his blue funk. But now he was glad to go with her. It was an old picture, but one he hadn't seen and had meant to see. He'd always loved Westerns when they were good, and this was one of the best. From time to time he glanced at Nora, not sure that she'd meant it when she said she liked them, too. But she seemed to be enjoying this one.

He felt better until the newsreels of the World Congress meeting were switched on. That was bad enough. But the riot that followed was worse. One of the smaller European nations had been backing up the United States at the World Congress. Some fanatic leader had whipped up the people against that, almost overnight, with wild warnings of the dangers of the stations, and there had been a near revolution against the leaders. Hundreds had been killed before the riots were put down.

It was a somewhat backward nation, and the people were probably superstitious about anything out of their usual experience. By itself, the news didn't mean much. But the reaction of the audience did. There was very little of the indignation Jim had expected when the fanatic's shouts were quoted.

Out on the street the newsboys were crying an extra, and Jim bought a paper. He drew back under the lights with Nora to read it.

The World Congress had finally voted, and the news was bad. They had ruled that orbits were free for anyone to use. But they'd gone further. They had ruled that no nation could have more than one extra- commercial station; it meant that the United States was limited to one, but the Combined People's States — theoretically a union of nations — could put up one for each of its members! And it also meant that the Combine had swung a lot of nations from the Alliance in the voting.

Jim walked back with Nora, discussing the news. He didn't even see Jonas in the lobby until the man caught his arm.

"You two are checking out on the next flight up," he told them, and his face was spread with the widest smile Jim had seen. "I've already had your things packed and waiting."

Jim held out the paper. "You mean you haven't seen the news?"

"Oh, that!" Jonas shoved the paper aside, still beaming. "It's ancient history by now. I've got later news. Kids, Congress just finished holding an emergency session. They not only reported our appropriation bill out of Committee, but they passed it and President Andrews has signed it. We've got the funds for the Moon trip!"

He told them a little about it as he drove them out to the rocket field. It had been the World Congress ruling that had decided things. Such an adverse decision couldn't be taken lying down. And if the United States had to take a back seat in number of permitted stations, Senator Blounce had pointed out, there was still one place where they could win. Nobody could build a second moon, and it was up to the United States to get there at once, now.

Obviously, the majority had agreed with him.

Chapter 6 - Full Speed Ahead

BACK AT THE STATION, there wasn't too much time for thinking, as work got under way. It was to be a rush job, now that it was finally started. Parts were being tooled out on Earth and rushed up, along with the great loads of fuel for the long trip. All the supply rockets were running on full schedule.

Jim buckled down to work, and gave up speculating on the strange ways of getting things done politically. It was obvious that the American spokesmen at the World Congress had deliberately worked against their own cause to get exactly the ruling that had come through; President Andrews must have planned the whole thing as the only way to get the appropriations passed. It was too tricky for Jim, but it had worked, and he didn't care how.

The first job was to bring back the old crew from the relay station. Work there was almost finished, and it could be completed before all the men would be needed for the Moon ships.

Jim brought the workers down, a few at a time. Most of them were delighted at the chance to sign on with the new job. They went to work at once, throwing up a big tank-like living quarters about fifteen miles beyond the station, where most of the building would be done. There wasn't room for them now in the station itself, but they were used to working without gravity and to roughing it. Dan Bailey had come back on the first trip and was supervising the building of the shack, as they called it.

Surprisingly, though, there were some who wouldn't be joining the new job. The appropriation had come too late. Worried by the fear of having nothing further to do in space, and tempted by fabulous contracts and salaries, a number of men and women had accepted bids for work on the Combine station.

One man explained it reluctantly to Jim. "Sure, I know it isn't good. But what could we do? Even with the Moon ships, our country won't have much more work up here. And by the time the Combine finishes all its stations, I'll be too old to work anyhow. So I signed on where I could stay in space." He sighed, though, as he said it, and his eyes went down toward the original station. "Wish I'd known they were building the Moon ships in time, all the same."

Still, with a trickle of new men, there would be enough. It wouldn't be as big a job as building the station had been.

Then the last of the men from the relay station were down, and Jonas came up to join Thorndyke in supervising the job of getting ready for the big leap. Jim turned the ferry back to its regular pilot who had recovered, and went for his assignment.

"You'll be one of the foremen, of course," Jonas told him. "I'll let you work on the cargo ship. Bailey will take one passenger ship and Terry Rodriguez has joined up to work on the other. I guess you've earned the foreman job."

But he seemed reluctant, and Jim remembered the doubts before about his ability to handle the men. Still, he'd handled them when they'd staged the "mutiny," and he knew them better than he had before.

He studied the plans again, along with Terry and Dan. There were to be three ships. Two would make the trip both ways, but the cargo ship would be meant to land on the Moon and stay there. All the ships were ugly things, compared to the sleek, streamlined rockets up from Earth. They would be big frameworks of girders, a hundred and sixty feet long and a little over a hundred feet wide. At the front, each would carry a big metal sphere for the crew. Below that, on the passenger ships, there would be huge cylindrical tanks for fuel, and the other end would be built up of banks of rocket motors, welded to a flat plate on which the landing legs would be fastened. The cargo ship, or tank, would have the same living sphere and motors, but its middle section would be similar to a big silo, filled with supplies for the stay on the Moon.

The main feature of all would be the "space balloons" that would hold most of the fuel for the takeoff. These would be four big nylon globes, held by a framework to the sides of each ship. Once the takeoff was finished, these would be tossed off into space. And it was on these that the work was to begin, since they would also serve as reservoirs for the fuel that would take countless trips from Earth to deliver.

They drew lots for the crewmen, with a few exceptions where requests had been made to work under Terry or Dan. Two men had applied for work under Jim, however, and that gave him some self-confidence.

They began assembling at once. Out here, there was no maze of girders to act as walkways yet. They had to move about almost entirely by the use of the tiny hand rockets they carried. A man had no leverage, usually. He could move a piece of metal or a folded strip of nylon, but he had to shove himself the other way at the same time. It was only by careful use of the hand rockets that progress could be made.

It was tough on the few new men, and tougher on Jim than he'd expected. Work was hard enough in the space suits, at best, but he hadn't realized how much he'd counted on the support he had originally received from the beginning framework of the station. Here, the experience of the men who had worked on the relay station gave them an edge.

But slowly the big balloons took shape. It was slower than the time schedule called for, and Jim studied the work, trying to drive his men on. He was doing twice as much as any of them at this stage, but it still seemed to crawl. Unconsciously, he'd been expecting them to work with the same fevered speed they had shown when finishing the station, but they somehow weren't doing it.

"You're pressing too hard, Jim," Dan told him. "You'll only get accidents that way."

Yet Dan's work was farther along than his, and so was Terry's. Jim buckled down, studying the work and trying to reduce it to its most efficient form. He found ways of sewing and cementing the sections together without more than half the usual motions, and he tried to get the others to follow. He wasn't too successful.

They'd formed habits already, and there were snags in trying to switch over.

Even then Terry beat him in getting the first balloon finished. Jim watched it being filled from the tanks of helium and tested for leaks. It was a good job. But he felt sick as he saw the large gaps in his own job.

The men could feel his reaction. He was trying to be fair, and he knew he couldn't force them to work as hard as he did. But his annoyance must have registered. He tried setting the pace, and he had to admit that they attempted to follow his lead. But it didn't seem to help.

Then a worker on his crew made a bad move with his rocket pistol, and sent its searing flame scorching against the fabric of the incomplete balloon. Without air, it couldn't burn, but the plastic nylon melted. A whole section was ruined, and they had to take time out to uncement it and replace it from the small supply of spare parts.

Jim held a meeting that night in the quarters, and was surprised to find that there was resentment because of that. All he wanted to do was to go over safety precautions with them and to try to lay out the work on a schedule they could keep. He was unprepared for the comment of one of the men.

"We can't all be supermen, Jim," the man said.

"Nobody expects you to be, Bill," Jim told him. "All I'm asking you to do is try things a different way. We can't risk any delay on this, and you all know that as well as I do. Until we're well along, we're running the danger that the Combine may jump the gun on us with a Moon trip of their own — or at least the announcement of one, to throw pressure against us. Are there any kicks?"

Bill shook his head glumly. "Nobody's kicking. We haven't forgotten the way we got along before. And if you have any kicks, we'll listen."

Jim couldn't object to that, and for a while he thought the meeting had been a success, But there was another accident the next day, and another. Whatever was needed to get smooth teamwork out of the men remained a mystery. Dan Bailey's crew finished their first balloon, found a minor leak, and corrected it. There was still a day's work ahead on the one Jim was supervising.

But at last it was finished, and they began blowing it up, coating it with a sprayed plastic film. Bubbles would form where there were any leaks, and the plastic would help to strengthen the balloon, even if it proved perfect.

Jim's face sagged as he watched. It looked as if there wasn't a seam without a leak! He jetted his way closer. It wasn't quite as bad as a total ruin, but it was worse than his darkest fears.

"All right," he told the men through the little radio in his helmet. "Knock off. We'll patch it up tomorrow." They said nothing as they coasted back to the living shack. But he could see the looks the other crews threw at them. It wasn't going to help any to have his men feel that they'd been the only crew to mess up a job.

"Guess I wasn't ready to be a foreman," he told Nora. "Maybe I'm a lone wolf. I can do a job, but I can't tell others to do it."

She patted his shoulder sympathetically, but he could see the worry thick in her expression. "It's your first try at it, Jim. You can't expect to build Rome in a day."

But Jim knew it wasn't just inexperience. He'd had experience in the final days of the station. And he couldn't see that he was doing anything differently now.

"Maybe that's the trouble," Nora suggested. "Maybe things aren't the same as they were when we were trying to prove to Jonas that he was wrong. Maybe this is just a job to the men, instead of a challenge."

"There isn't a man out there who doesn't want the Moon trip as much as I do!" Jim told her.

"Maybe. But maybe they don't feel there's all the rush about it as much as you do. Why don't you see Mr. Jonas?"

It was the only thing he could do. The taxi had already gone back to the station, which meant he'd have to make it without assistance. But he stood up and began buckling on his suit again. "You're right. I'd better see him."

"Now?" she asked. She frowned doubtfully. "At least you can wait while we radio the taxi. Jim, I don't like your making the jump. If you miss . . ."

He shook his head. "I won't miss. And it's quicker this way."

He snapped his helmet shut before she could protest further and headed for the lock, gathering up several of the hand rockets on the way. Outside, he lined himself up carefully and blasted off toward the station. Handling the little rockets was tricky, since every motion in space was like skating on completely frictionless ice, but he was used to that. He watched his progress from the first blast and made a careful correction. Out here, anything in motion tended to stay at the same speed and in the same direction forever, unless acted on by some other force. He watched the station come nearer rapidly, but his thoughts were on the interview.

It wasn't pleasant to have to confess failure, but he had to face facts, pleasant or not. He had failed. He corrected for a landing and used a counterblast to slow until he could grab a handrail. The hub attendant opened the lock for him and helped him off with his suit.

Jonas was in the commissary when Jim located him. He looked up in surprise and then waved the younger man to a table opposite him. "Hi, Jim. I was just thinking of taxiing over to see you. Glad you saved me a trip. I heard you had a little trouble."

"I made a botch of things, sir. And I don't know why!"

The other nodded. "I was afraid that might happen. You've been developing a lot from the self-centered, unsocial kid you were a year ago. But I didn't think you were ready to lead a crew yet. How old are you, Jim?"

"Nineteen."

"Yeah. That makes you younger than a lot of the men you're giving orders to. It makes things a little tougher. Terry's no older, of course, but he's used to working with labor gangs. Know what the trouble is?" At Jim's puzzled headshake, Jonas pushed back his coffee and went on. "You can't delegate work. You can't realize yet that people have differences and trust them to get things done if you let them pick their own speed. You still think like a young rebel, at war with a timetable. Maybe it works for you, but under these circumstances, it won't work for others."

"But I've tried to relax," Jim protested. "I don't want to be tough on anyone."

"You are, though. The men know when you're dissatisfied. They see you take the tough jobs yourself because you don't trust them. As a young fighter against hopeless odds, you were terrific, Jim. But you can't force men to join a rebellion against that timetable; they can't see it the way you do — and maybe they're right. . . So what am I going to do with you?"

"Fire me, I suppose," Jim said bitterly.

But it came as a shock when Jonas nodded. "You're right. I can't do anything else. I'll put Thorndyke out with your men — he learned a lot on the relay job. And you can take over the taxi jockeying again, where you're the best man, anyhow."

Jim stood up abruptly. "Sorry I failed."

"You didn't fail. I just gave you a job you weren't ready for. Sometimes it pays, in the long run. Get the taxi and take it back with you. And next time, Jim, don't wait so long to come to me with your troubles!"

Jim stumbled back up the spoke to the hub and into the little space taxi. He hadn't realized how much he'd counted on proving that he'd learned enough to fill the job. He wasn't used to failing.

Chapter 7 - Crackup!

JIM got used to the idea in the days that followed. The ships began growing as the balloons were finished and construction was started on the framework. Once the idea of streamlining was forgotten, the ships had a certain functional beauty. Even the naked track, on which were to be mounted the solar mirror for power, the radar screen, and the unloading cranes, seemed to fit into the general lines.

Surprisingly, nobody laughed at Jim's demotion. The men of his crew seemed relieved, but now they spoke to him more freely, as if he were one of them. Sometimes, when there was no need for taxiing supplies from the ships to the materials base, he went out to work with Thorndyke's crew. They were back on schedule once more, and Jim could feel some satisfaction in that. But his one big relief came from finding his name still on the list of pilots for the Moon ships. Everyone was too busy to worry about the Combine, mercifully, and there was little news, beyond the fact that the second big station was proceeding rapidly. Most of Jim's worries involved young Freddy Halpern. The boy's father had consented to let him learn to use the taxi, and Jim had been teaching him to pilot, with the help of some of the microfilms. But keeping an eye on him was more of a job than it should have been.

Freddy was curious about everything, and he had to try anything the others were doing. Sometimes, when Jim's back was turned, the boy would disappear among the men, trying to appear part of the crew. Thorndyke didn't seem to mind, but Jim was worried. There were too many chances for carelessness to result in death here; it took only a small hole in a suit to kill a man. And Freddy was far too unconcerned with danger.

But they got along well enough, on the whole.

It was Freddy who told Jim the next news of the relations between the Combine and the United States. Mark Emmett's ship was just pulling up from Earth, bound for the station, and Jim was getting ready to meet it when the boy joined him.

"I'll bet it's that foreign spy," he said. "Dad got word he was coming up today. Right on the ship, as if he belonged here!"

On the trip to the rocket Jim got most of what the boy knew out of him. It seemed that the Combine and the United States had reached an agreement to exchange scientists, just as ambassadors had been exchanged of old. The two nations were operating on a level of good relations, on the surface. It was logical enough for them to exchange scientists in the stations, at that, and probably the best way to quiet some of the fears below.

But Jim shared some of Freddy's worries, even after he delivered the man who had come up on the rocket. Halpern was in the hub to greet the short, dark-skinned man who pulled off the odd-looking space suit, and he made the introductions. "Dr. Charkejian, this is Jim Stanley. You may have heard of him."

The scientist smiled, and his voice was low and pleasant as he replied in perfect English. "Indeed I have. I was told to look you up, Jim. In fact, Director Chiam sent his personal regards and a small token of his esteem."

He opened the small bag he carried and drew out a book, which he passed over. Jim stared at it unbelievingly. It was a first-edition copy of Hermann Oberth's *The Rocket into Interplanetary Space.* Since the success of space flight, it had become one of the most valuable books in existence, and this was something any rocketman could appreciate. Inside was an inscription from Peter Chiam, expressing his gratitude for his rescue and the hope that someday he and Jim might meet under happier circumstances.

Halpern studied it, frowning. If word of it got out, Jim could see that it might mean more rumors about too much fraternizing here. He wondered briefly if that were what was intended. But then pleasure in the gift overcame his doubts.

Surprisingly, the scientists aboard the station accepted Charkejian without much question. Apparently the man was one of the world's greatest astrophysicists, and they considered it perfectly proper that he would want to be up here, where the seeing was always perfect without the haze of atmosphere.

Jim couldn't feel quite as happy. "It still doesn't mean he

isn't a spy," he told Nora. "Oh, I know Freddy was just romanticizing things. But Charkejian could be more than he seems."

"You've got problems enough without taking on the whole world," she chided him. "Let the screening boards down on Earth take care of a few things, Jim. You've got enough to do to keep your own eyes on Freddy!"

Jim nodded. But he was growing used to the boy, and quite pleased with what Freddy was learning. He had the makings of a good pilot, and a surprisingly keen mind for the mathematics of plotting a course. By now Freddy could probably handle the trip up to the relay station alone, without trouble.

Then the next day Freddy found out that Jim was supposed to watch him. He overheard a bit of conversation between Jim and the colonel and guessed the rest. From then on, he seemed to take his greatest delight in slipping away from Jim's care. It kept Jim hopping, but he was less worried now, since the boy seemed to be learning to handle himself in space.

The ships were coming along rapidly. The big girders were being put together and the solar mirrors were already functioning, concentrating the heat on a tube of mercury that boiled and drove a turbine generator. It made work easier, since there was now full power for the construction work.

The cargo ship was Jim's pet. He had found that it was the ship which he'd probably pilot, and he went over it again and again as it was assembled, working on it every free moment. Its big silo-hull was just taking form, leaving huge storage bins for the supplies. The cylinder would serve a double purpose. It would hold food, water, oxygen and everything else the men would need on the Moon. And after the landing, it could be split into two sections, like big Quonset huts, and set up on the surface as living quarters.

Ten men would go with the cargo ship and twenty with each of the other ships. In addition to the men, the passenger ships would have fourteen tanks of fuel for the return trip and for the landing on the Moon, located where the supply hull was on the cargo ship.

Materials continued to come up, and there were times when Jim worked long hours overtime, stacking them in the supply dump. At that, his constant striving for perfection was useful. The men had

51

taken it for granted that supplies would be dumped hither and thither, but they appreciated it when they found he was careful to line up girders in such a way that matching sections caught the sun in the same manner. And they were even more pleased when they saw that he kept a careful eye on construction progress and made sure the material they needed first would be closest to them.

He was working with Bill Carr on one occasion when the taxi was idle, welding together the girders that connected the passenger sphere to the rocket motor platform. It was then that he caught the first feeling of their complete acceptance of him. Bill glanced at Thorndyke's back, where the foreman was laying out the next day's work, and jerked a heavy-mittened hand toward him.

"Good guy," Bill said over his phones. "But you're making his work a snap, the way you pile things, Jim. Wish we'd had a man like you at the relay station. Coming to the dance?"

"Dance?" Jim asked. It was the first he'd heard of it.

"Sure. Something we invented at the relay. Come on over to our section of the shack tonight and bring Nora along."

Nora was eager to go and filled with curiosity. She knew as well as Jim that dancing was impossible without gravity, but a party was a party. From Jim's view, he was glad it couldn't be a real dance; dancing was one of the social graces he'd never had a chance to learn.

It turned out to be one of the best evenings for a long time. They had a tiny tape player and some music for it. Men and women paired off, a few starting the activity. They let themselves drift across a part of the shack from which they had cleared the cloth partitions, trying to time their flight to the music. As others joined, it became a game of jostling from couple to couple. It was sort of a cross between square dancing and jitterbugging, as it turned out. And they'd even evolved a few maneuvers that could be done in patterns.

Jim was awkward at first when those started. But the boy doing the calling came sailing over to help, and Nora caught on quickly. Jim watched her go sailing from partner to partner before the maneuvers brought her back to him, laughing as she went.

Jonas had come to watch, along with Halpern, but they kept in the background, and left early. They apparently knew that officials couldn't really mix too freely with the crew. But before they left, Jonas motioned Jim to him.

"Find out who started all this, will you, Jim? It's the best idea we've had up here. I'd like that kind of man on the Moon trip, even if I have to leave out some scientist the government has chosen to send."

Jim was tired but happier than he'd been for a long time when the evening broke up, and more determined than ever to get along with the men around him. He had long since learned that keeping to himself didn't pay — and now maybe he was learning how to get along with the others. The fact that he'd been invited made it seem that way.

There was more work accomplished the next day, too, he noticed. Apparently the relaxation had been good in every way. He finished his ferrying early, looked up the rocket schedule, and found that bad weather would ground the ships for the next twenty-four hours. The station hadn't solved all the problems of long-range weather predicting yet, but it was well on the way. The scientists could already read the movement of the cloud masses below well enough to be pretty sure of the weather for a few days ahead.

Jim wondered how many farmers would realize the warnings that saved their crops had come from space. It was easy to take things for granted. Then he forgot it as he put on his working suit and prepared to go out to join the crew.

Freddy was already out there, about equally helpful and a nuisance, but Thorndyke liked the boy, and seemed to get on well with him. Freddy was busy with the job of moving small sections of piping across to where the men working the crude cranes could line up the pipe for welding, and he obviously considered himself a man among men. Jim grinned, but let the boy alone, as he knew Freddy wanted. He saw that Bill was working one of the torsion bars into place further along the ship, but the man already had a helper. It didn't matter. There was still the job of bolting down sections of the rocket platform, and there he could be fully useful.

Jim collected the tools and the belt that would hold him in place, and began bolting down. It was monotonous work, but it gave him a good feeling to see plate after plate drop into place as he moved along.

The shift was almost over before he knew it. He finished the final plate, stowed his tools away, and began unfastening his belt.

Then a yell went up in his phones. He jerked around, instinctively catching a handhold to keep from overturning, and stared. The yell had come from Thorndyke.

"Timber! Timber! Fred, get out of there!"

The cry of "timber" had been carried over from other work, and it meant something heavy heading for someone. Jim jerked his eyes around. Nothing was moving except the big torsion bar Bill was working on. It had apparently been fastened to its pivot at one end, and Bill was now using the crane engine to swing it into place.

Then Jim saw the small figure of Freddy near it. The boy had a load of plates and was rocketing along with his hand motor, not looking. He must have either forgotten to renew his radio battery or had it turned off, because he gave no sign of having heard Thorndyke's yell.

Bill was frantically trying to kill the momentum of the big bar, but that took time, and there wasn't enough time left. In a second, Freddy would strike the end of the bar. The fabric of the space suits wasn't designed to take that kind of punishment.

Jim's legs bent under him, while his arms forced his body down to hold contact with the platform. Then he took quick aim and leaped.

Freddy glanced at him, and suddenly swiveled his head toward the bar lunging toward him. It would be close, Jim knew, but if he could hit the boy in time and knock him out of the way . . .

Freddy's mouth opened as if he were screaming, and the pile of plates sailed from his arms. With a jerk, he had his hand rocket out and began blasting away from the coming danger.

Jim saw him clear the end of the bar by inches and breathed a quick sigh of relief. Then Thorndyke's voice yelled again. "Jim! TIMBER!"

But it was too late for Jim to do anything. He sailed by the place where Freddy would have been, straight toward the big bar. At the last second, he managed to flip partway over, trying to take the impact on the thick soles of his boots.

He didn't quite make it. Something hit with agony against his shin, and he could hear the bone snap! Then the leg went numb as he sailed toward Thorndyke, who was leaping out to catch him.

There was still air in his suit, so it hadn't been punctured. But his leg was completely useless.

Chapter 8 - Washout

NORA brought out the taxi and ferried Jim back to the station infirmary, careful not to disturb his leg until Dr. Perez could look at it. The numbness was wearing off by the time they reached the station, and pain was shooting up Jim's leg with every slight movement.

He saw Nora's white face as she stripped from her suit and joined the doctor in cutting the cloth away from the injured leg. Jim looked down, seeing the ugly discoloration. The leg seemed to dangle.

"Simple fracture. Green-splint, I guess," Perez reported after a quick examination. "It could be worse. Of course, we'll know better when we make a gamma picture of the bone. But I think you're lucky, Jim. Hurt?"

It hurt more than he could say, but he tried to grin. "A little."

"We'll fix that," Perez told him. There was a hypo in the doctor's hand, and he injected something quickly. The pain began to go away, and Jim's mind seemed to disconnect itself. He tried to tell Nora not to worry about him, but it was too much effort. He made no attempt to fight against the sleepiness, however, knowing that it was best for him. Within minutes he was unconscious.

When he came to again, he was lying by himself, with the leg bound up and braced carefully on the hammock. He could see metal braces. The drug had saved him any feeling of the agony of having the bone set. The worst was already over, and he was lucky to have escaped so lightly.

Then he sobered, as his thoughts began exploring what it would mean. It took time to realize he was a cripple! He wouldn't be able to work the taxi or to help with the building of the ships. Worse than that, he certainly couldn't do any piloting with a bad leg. And if the trip to the Moon went on schedule . . .

Nora came in then, back in her nurse's uniform. She seemed surprised to see him awake, but she looked cheerful. "It was a simple fracture, Jim. Perez says it'll mend so well that you'll never realize it was broken. So cheer up!"

"I'm all right," he told her.

But when she left to take over his job with the taxi, he lay in a dark cloud of gloom. He would probably be sent back to Earth now. He was no use in space, and he was taking up room and attention that would have been better used for workers. He'd made a complete fool of himself.

He hadn't stopped to think. When Freddy first reached for his hand rocket, Jim should have known that the boy could avoid the bar, and have reached for his own. There would have been time enough, but he had been so busy watching Freddy that he hadn't paid enough attention to his own situation. The very thing for which he'd so often lectured Freddy!

He had a stream of visitors, among them Freddy, who was full of contrition at first. But he recovered quickly enough when he found Jim wasn't angry at him, his mind full of the latest developments. "They've started work on the survey ship, Jim! And Dad was talking with Mr. Jonas about it, so I got the whole picture. They'll be starting in two weeks!"

Jim hadn't thought of the survey ship, but the news jolted him. He'd known about it, but had overlooked it in the haste to finish the main ships. The little survey rocket would be something like the ferry to the relay station, though a little bigger and more powerful. It wasn't designed to land on the Moon, but to circle around it and back, taking pictures and making a survey of the surface to help in determining the best spot for the final landing.

And the man who piloted it would be the first human being to see the other side of the Moon!

After Freddy left, Jim lay speculating bitterly about that. He was pretty sure Jonas would have let him be the pilot, under normal conditions. His familiarity with the ferry and taxi would be in his favor.

Now he was a washup, and all that was impossible! In two weeks, he was sure, he wouldn't be permitted to leave. When he questioned Perez, the doctor confirmed it. Jim would be practically useless for longer than that. On Earth, he could have been moving around on a crutch by now, but Perez had forbidden him to get up for a few days. Men were less conscious of their legs where the gravity was lower, and the doctor couldn't be responsible for what might happen.

Jim fretted and fumed to himself, though he tried to keep up a good act when there were others around.

Bill and Thorndyke dropped around, and even Dr. Charkejian came to express his sympathies. But Jim didn't want sympathy. He wanted a chance to be on the survey ship. He was torn between pleasure and envy when he heard how quickly the work on it was being done.

The fourth day they moved him to a stretcher, and Nora and Dr. Perez carried him up into the hub, where a sling had been prepared for him.

"It's Nora's idea," Dr. Perez said. "She's been studying the work being done on cell growth without gravity, and she thinks your bone may knit faster here where there's no spin. Besides, you're less apt to hurt yourself if you keep twisting and turning."

"How much faster could it heal?" Jim asked.

"We don't know. This is just an experiment," the doctor answered. "But if you're so impatient, you might try being more cheerful. It usually promotes healing."

Jim thought he'd acted as cheerful as he could, but he made no protest.

It was in the hub that Jonas visited him. The man came in, staring down at Jim and shaking his head. There was no optimistic nonsense about him. He studied Jim, and then snorted. "You're a problem, boy!"

"I don't want to be," Jim told him. "But if I'm in the way . . ."

"I didn't mean that. I meant your attitude. You act as if a broken leg is the end of the world. I'm afraid you're one of the pioneer types we keep hearing about. You won't be content to plod along like the average man. And you can't turn adventure into a game. You're no hero — as I suspect Mark Emmett is. No, you have to be the type who stays at the frontiers where the adventure is, but takes it all as seriously as death and taxation."

"I'm sorry, Mr. Jonas. But I've tried to change."

The supervisor snorted again. "And you get so darned serious about that, too! Look, nobody wants you to change. We're going to need all types. There's room out here for the heroic adventurer, and someday we'll need the men who consider it business, not adventure. But I suspect you're the kind who'll settle the Moon and make it habitable someday — when you grow up enough to take your troubles as something that won't last forever. Stop sweating and stewing. The world isn't coming to an end today!"

"Then get me out of here," Jim suggested. "They put me here to get me out of gravity. But there's no gravity pull on the construction site, either. I can do paper work, or something."

"I'll see what I can do," Jonas promised. "I guess you make a little sense there, at that. Only stop trying so hard at everything you do!"

"I'll try," Jim said. And then, at Jonas' grin, he realized he'd fallen into a trap. But how could a man stop trying too hard without working hard at it?

Perez fussed and fumed, examining the leg, but at last he nodded. "You're healing splendidly. I think it's probably going at least twice the usual rate. All right, I'll let you go out if you'll promise to be careful."

Jim was more than willing to be careful. He tried to find out when healing would be finished enough for him to return to full duty, but the doctor wouldn't commit himself. It might be within the two weeks, he admitted — but it might not.

Still, it felt good going back. Nora moved the taxi as if the slightest acceleration would crush him, but he didn't feel a thing. And Thorndyke seemed glad to have him take over the work of checking off progress against the charts and keeping track of supplies. It was awkward getting about with only his hands, but he learned the trick, and was even able to get outside the shack, once he was helped into his space suit.

The survey ship was coming along rapidly. It was enough like the ferry to present no special problems, and a gang of ten men was enough to push it through — which made for more closely co-ordinated work. Thorndyke let Jim supervise most of what remained.

Jim found that being unable to do any of the work himself was a help rather than a hindrance. It made it easier to consider the other men's jobs.

The survey ship would consist of three globes, fastened together with light girders, with a converted motor from one of the third stages at the rear. Two of the big globes would hold the hydrazine and nitric acid, while the front globe would contain all supplies for the ten-day trip, as well as the cameras needed for the survey mapping.

Now Jim began to hope. Dr. Perez examined him every second day, clucking happily over the healing. Apparently the doctor was busy writing a paper on it for some medical journal, and as excited over that as Jim was about the ships.

"When?" Jim asked him again.

This time Perez grinned, instead of putting him off. "By the time you've finished the survey ship, Jim; that last gamma picture shows the bone all knit right now. I just want it to have a little more time. Then some exercise to make up for all this inactivity — though that isn't as important out here as it would be on Earth." Perez grinned again. "Now are you satisfied?"

Jim was more than satisfied. He got Perez' promise that the doctor would report on his condition to Jonas and went back to work, happier than he had been for a long time. He still couldn't be sure that he'd be the one selected for the trip. They might decide on a lottery. But. . .

He realized then that he didn't even know who the other pilots would be. But Thorndyke had the answer to that. "You, of course. And then Gantry and Mark."

"Gantry?"

"He's on the list."

It was a surprise. But as Jim considered it, less of a surprise than it might have been. Somehow Gantry had done it again. Out of the list of pilots with everything in their favor, he'd managed to prove his ability in spite of weight and age. Jim was glad for him.

"Gantry'll be in command, among the three of you," Thorndyke volunteered. "Or so I hear."

"Does that mean he'll get first chance at taking the survey

ship out?"

Thorndyke stared in surprise, and then shook his head. "I guess they didn't tell you anything, Jim, while they had you strapped down. Come along. Hey, easy! Want to break a leg again?"

Jim relaxed. It seemed harder now for him to remember his leg than for others — probably because the splints served as a visible reminder for them. It felt almost as good as ever. He let Thorndyke help him into his suit, and they drifted over to the pile of material for the survey ship, where Thorndyke pointed.

"The big crate," the foreman said over the phones.

It had been pried open already, and some of the bracing had been removed, indicating the men were about ready to install it. Jim stared at it doubtfully, thinking at first that it was an automatic mapping camera. Then he caught sight of the wiring diagram etched into it. It was a maze of transistors and electronic parts, with what seemed to be space for miles of control tape.

"It looks a little like an automatic pilot," he said. Then he stared again, realizing that it must be exactly that. But there was no reason to use an automatic on this job. Unless . . .

"You're right," Thorndyke told him. The foreman's body jiggled about under his head as he nodded, compensating for the motion; but it was easier to grow used to that than to break the habit of making gestures. "The Army's come up with a control system they think foolproof, and they've sent it out for the trip. There won't be any other pilot on this."

"But Jonas told me there would. That's why they bothered with the oxygen and food supplies for this ship," Jim protested.

"Jonas had nothing to do with it," Thorndyke said. "It came through Halpern. Don't forget that this whole expedition may be in civilian hands, but the government's footing the bill, and what they say goes."

Jim stared down at the metal monster that had replaced him. He could admire it, and realize how important such devices might be someday. But right now, he was almost ready to hate it. Then he squared his shoulders.

It hadn't beaten him yet. If a man like Gantry could win a place as head of the big jump when he was considered a hundred pounds too heavy and twenty years too old, there was always a chance. And at least the metal device couldn't fight back.

Besides, Halpern owed him a favor for his watching over Freddy. He'd never expected to ask repayment, but this situation had changed all that.

He had to see Halpern, and the sooner the better.

Chapter 9 - Automatic Computer

JIM found the colonel in his office, together with Dr. Charkejian and one of the station scientists. There was quite a to-do made over Jim's leg, but the others were just leaving, and Jim waited until they were gone. Then Halpern shoved a cup across to him and poured coffee.

"Glad you can get around, Jim. I was about ready to ground Freddy for good, after what happened."

"It wasn't really his fault," Jim protested.

"I hope not. Umm, know what Charkejian and Moss have done? You might be interested in it. They've put together bits of our science with that of the Combine and come up with a method for making a positive identification of living vegetation under sunlight. And they've found that there's some form of life around the canals we've finally succeeded in photographing on Mars. Proof of it!"

No piece of purely theoretical science could have meant more. It had been good to have proof that there were canals on Mars — though they couldn't know what made them — but the knowledge of other life in the solar system was even better. It made a trip to Mars in the future almost certain.

But at the moment, Jim's mind was too filled with the nearer trip, and Halpern seemed to sense it. "What's up, Jim? You look as if you wanted something. I owe you quite a bit, so ask away."

His face sobered as he listened to Jim's request to go in place of the automatic computer. He shook his head, when Jim was finished.

"I'd be glad to, Jim, if I had the authority. But it's out of my hands." He made a vague gesture toward Earth below them. "Down there they feel we'll learn more with a chance to test their robot brain. And they don't want to risk sending a man that far out until they know more about conditions. With the brain there and radio controls from here, they figure the trip can be purely unmanned."

"Sure, I suppose they could do it," Jim agreed. "But why take

63

chances? Maybe a robot brain can do a better job of piloting than I can. But suppose something goes wrong. Suppose it should hit a meteorite? A man could patch the hull and correct any error in the course. But this thing couldn't. Anyhow, radar contact is no good, once it gets to the other side of the Moon."

"All that was argued out down there by both sides. I have to operate on the orders I have," Halpern said. It was clearly a flat denial.

"But suppose you had a volunteer? They wouldn't have to take the responsibility in my case."

Halpern shook his head. "I'll put it up to the higher authorities again, but I don't think you have a chance. Anything else I can do for you?"

There wasn't, as far as Jim was concerned. He left as soon as he could and headed back toward the hub, until he heard his name being called. It was Dr. Ernst Charkejian.

"Why the scowl, Jim Stanley?" he asked. "I could see it all the way from the commissary."

Jim considered, still uncertain of the man's position here. He seemed to be completely accepted, and to be working with no thought of national rivalries. But there was no positive proof. Then Jim realized it didn't matter. The knowledge of the trip was spread thoroughly by now, and what he might do was of no great concern.

Charkejian listened sympathetically. When Jim was finished, he considered it. "Looks bad for you, eh? Umm. I'd say your best chance lies with the idea of the meteor hit. And there isn't too much chance of that. Still. . . Like to have me estimate the possibility of a hit and give it to the colonel? And I might be able to shade it a bit in your favor. I guess my reputation can stand that much strain."

"But why should you?" Jim asked, before realizing it might sound wrong.

Charkejian grinned, taking no offense. "Why not? I think you know that men have to get along in space and in science. Well, I know it too. Back on Earth we might be against each other someday. But up here, I'd rather be friends. Okay?"

It was more than okay with Jim. And some of his suspicion vanished.

He heard later through Freddy that Charkejian kept his word, bringing a long report to the colonel the next day, in which he proved that there was a chance for such a meteorite collision. But apparently it fell on deaf ears below. Freddy brought out a note from the astrophysicist, in which the man admitted that his report had done no good.

"But keep up hopes," the note finished. "I am still doing what I can to see that man shall not be replaced by robots!"

His written speech was stilted, unlike his spoken English. It was an odd reversal from the normal, until Jim realized that it probably came from the heavy tone of scientific writing, rather than from Charkejian's native tongue.

Jim forgot the note then. No matter how well Charkejian meant, what could he do? If Halpern couldn't convince the authorities, there was no chance for another man — and one from the Combine — to change their minds. Jim's first flush of determination had long since vanished.

But robot or man, something had to guide the ship around the Moon, and the sooner that was finished, the nearer they would be to the real trip. Perez finally admitted that Jim's leg was back to normal, and Jim pitched into the job of getting the little ship finished. The automatic computer hadn't been installed yet — that would have to be done by a specialist from Earth — nor had the supplies for the human pilot been removed. Jim was putting that off until the final moment, still nursing a few vague hopes.

Freddy seemed to be settling down and learning more all the time. Jim and Nora were beginning to grow fond of the boy, as Thorndyke seemed to be. Freddy was doing most of the taxi jockeying now, leaving Jim free to work on the survey ship, and he was doing a good job.

"Charkejian's been writing to the big shot over there," the boy reported to Jim. "Dad has to censor all his reports, so I know. And the last letter was all about you and how you want to take the ship to the Moon. You think it's some code, or is he really interested?"

"I think he's on the level," Jim answered, with only a small doubt. He couldn't see much use in filling up pages for Peter Chiam with his troubles. But there was no use in using them to fill in a code, either. "Does your father know you have to tell everything you hear, Freddy?"

The boy laughed. "Oh, he kicks me out when there's any really secret stuff. That's why I know I don't have to worry about the rest. Jim, is there room for two on that ship? Because I'd be glad to help you pilot it."

"When we get that robot in, there won't be room for one," Jim told him. There was room enough for three or four now, but he didn't want the boy building up false hopes. He'd had enough experience of his own with what happened when they broke.

Jonas came out to inspect the ship, more from interest than any official duty, when they finished with everything but the removal of the supplies to make room for the automatic computer. He had learned to handle himself fairly well in space, though he could never become as proficient as a younger man with less firmly fixed habits.

"It looks like a nice job, Jim," he said. "And maybe you're learning. Thorndyke tells me you supervised this without any trouble."

Jim hadn't thought too much about it, but he realized that the men had followed his suggestions automatically, and that they were nearly a day ahead of schedule. It felt good, though he knew the fact that he'd been crippled had made it easier at first, and that handling ten men was easier than running a whole crew.

"I suppose we'll have to get things ready for the computer?" he asked finally.

But Jonas didn't nod as he'd expected. The older man stared at the packaged mechanical brain doubtfully. "I don't know, Jim. I'd wait. There are new developments. Something's been buzzing behind the scenes at the World Congress, and they've put in a request to have a neutral observer aboard the ship when it rounds the Moon. They've got a young Swiss who has passed all the tests, too. Maybe you'd better leave it alone until we see what happens."

"You mean there's still a chance?" Jim asked.

"No — I don't know. Their request was based on the fact that this would be automatically piloted, and that Pierotti — that's the name of the man — was willing to accept the discomforts. But you'd better leave the supplies in, anyhow."

But later, when Jim visited the station to get more news, Halpern confirmed the fact that permission had been given, finally. He was surprised, and doubtful of the whole thing, but apparently the efforts to keep the good will of the smaller nations required that the government should give in on this request.

Pierotti arrived the next trip up. By then the newspapers had learned enough about him to know that he was a highly skilled international lawyer and mediator who had had a fair part in a number of settlements between countries. But from the way he managed to handle himself in space, Jim suspected that he'd gotten some rocket experience somewhere. He was of medium height, but very slender and wiry.

Jim liked him, and he noticed that Mark Emmett had already reached a friendly basis with the man. Pierotti's English was marred by only a slight tendency to make most of the sounds too clearly, but nobody noticed after the first few minutes.

Halpern greeted him and made him at home, before retiring with the official mail Mark had brought up. Jim was heading back for the taxi when Halpern's aide came running after him, summoning him back.

Charkejian was in Halpern's office, grinning as if he'd just won one of the long chess games he frequently played. The colonel was frowning. Now he tossed over one of the letters.

"Permission has been granted at the request of the Combine for them to have a man on the survey," he said. "And they've picked Dr. Charkejian. I don't know how much pressure was used, but it must have been plenty. Jim, did you have anything to do with this — did you put Dr. Charkejian up to it?"

Charkejian laughed and shook his head at Jim. "Not in any way he knew," he answered. "It's true, I appealed indirectly to our leader for him. And with world conditions as they are, I thought it might be possible for your government to grant our requests, rather than staging any debates. There are many things that can be done when two nations are going through a lull in their hostility. I felt sure our leader would guess my thought."

67

"Apparently it worked. Maybe you should have been in the diplomatic corps," Halpern said. But he seemed less annoyed now.

"I was," Charkejian told him. "For quite a few years. And I've attended a good many international scientific congresses. A man gets to know some of the ropes that way."

Jim couldn't see any sense in it. Nor could he see where he was mixed up in it. "What good would it have done me to suggest this, even if I'd thought of it, Colonel Halpern?"

Charkejian laughed again. "Jim, do you think your government is going to let the two of us — Pierotti and myself — go on that ship without making sure they've got one of their own citizens there? I'm sure Colonel Halpern can answer that."

"We're sending a pilot, of course," Halpern agreed. "I have orders for three men to go. But I still can't get your angle on this, Dr. Charkejian."

The scientist leaned back against his chair, half closing his eyes. "You never grew up in the slums of my little native town, then, looking at the stars my ancestors first named five thousand years ago, and dreamed as I dreamed. I *want* to go. And besides, I never told you I wasn't loyal to my own country. When Director Chiam asked me to make all attempts to repay Jim Stanley for his rescue, I accepted that as part of my job here. Chiam comes from a people who feel the obligation of a favor very deeply, Colonel Halpern. And he hasn't lost that, though he's adopted most of the rest of civilization. When Jim wanted to go on that trip, it was my duty to try every way to make sure he went." He paused, then smiled. "Besides, it's to our advantage to have this an international trip, rather than a purely American one. Maybe to the advantage of the world. It won't hurt the people to see international co-operation here."

Reluctantly, Halpern nodded.

"All right," he decided, "I'll buy that as a good reason, unofficially. And I'm glad to see human beings on the trip instead of an automatic computer."

He nodded to Jim. "You've been chosen as pilot, Stanley. And your course calls for takeoff day after tomorrow. You're in complete command, and under no obligation to accept any

68

suggestions from the others, though you'll be responsible for their safety."

Charkejian followed Jim into the hall, chuckling softly. "We still have an automatic computer, Jim," he said. "The best one ever created, and the only one that can handle unplanned emergencies — the human brain. Don't ever underrate it!" He let the chuckle creep back again, well pleased with himself. "If you're surprised by all this, Jim, so am I! I never thought Chiam would be able to put it over!"

Jim still couldn't believe it as he went back to his quarters. He was almost sure that after such good luck, something terrible was bound to happen. He knew it was superstition, but he'd been unable to shake the idea of having to pay for all good luck, and it bothered him now.

Chapter 10 - Once Around the Moon

THE ONLY TROUBLE came from Freddy. He was delighted when he learned Jim would pilot the ship — and sure that Jim would find some way for him to go along.

"You can't be alone with a Combine man and somebody else we don't even know," he said seriously.

"Suppose they decide to steal the ship and land on the Moon? They could claim it for the Combine, and then where'd we be?"

"You've read too many comic books," Jim accused him. "In the first place, Pierotti's a neutral, and if Charkejian tried anything, he'd have to help me. Then it wouldn't do any good to land — there wouldn't be enough fuel for takeoff again. Besides, I can't take you — and that's final, Freddy!"

"How can you stop me if I stow away?"

Jim found nothing funny in the idea. There was too much chance that the kid might try it. And while it seemed impossible for him to find any hiding place, Jim didn't want to have to go looking for him.

"Try it if you like, Freddy. But if you do, and if you succeed, do you know what I'll have to do? And I'm not joking about this, either!"

"What?"

"I'd have to dump you," Jim told him. It was the truth, too, he realized as he said it. "With the ship carrying just enough oxygen for three men, your going along would mean we'd run out of air before we got back. I'd have to put you into your suit — or maybe just the way you are — and shove you out through the airlock."

"Why not Charkejian?" The boy was studying Jim's face, and the humor drained out of him as he saw that Jim meant what he had said.

"Because I'm responsible for Charkejian, but not for a stowaway. The two men belong there. You don't. Without official orders, I can't take you."

"All right then, let them steal the Moon from us!" Freddy was bitter. He stomped off, probably to bother his father.

Jim found out later that he'd guessed right about that. It must have been a rough job, convincing the boy that he couldn't have the one thing he wanted most. But apparently it was settled when Halpern finally gave his son permission to take command of the ferry up to the relay station. He made sure from Jim that the boy could handle it, and then gave in. But Jim had little time to worry about Freddy as he supervised the installation of the extra supplies they would need for three. The little globe was going to be a tight squeeze now, but they could stand it for ten days.

Charkejian and Pierotti were out, getting familiar with space and free fall conditions. There wasn't much question about the Swiss observer. He seemed to take to space naturally. But Charkejian was having a tough time. It was always harder for older people.

"It's purely mental," he gasped once as Jim suggested he go back and rest. "The body can handle it. But habits keep making me think I'm falling. I'll be all right."

Jim wasn't so sure. Less than one out of three could learn to stand space, and that included much younger men. "You'd better rest for a while," he suggested again.

The scientist shook his head, gasping as his body jerked. "I tell you it isn't physical, Jim. I can't rest my brain — I've got to make it accept the facts, that's all."

Whether his theory was right or not, he began to improve. He obviously suffered horribly at first, and his body lost nearly five pounds. But in the end even Jim could find no fault with the way he reacted.

Their course had been plotted precisely, second by second. It had to be done by rule now, not by feel.

The trip would take five days to the Moon, and they had to aim at a spot where the satellite would be at the end of that time, rather than heading straight for the ball they could see. Then they had to depend on the pull of the Moon to swing them around and send them back — again on a precisely figured course.

The whole staff was out to watch the three men as they finally pulled themselves into the little globe and tested it. Jim spotted Freddy in the group watching and breathed more easily. He'd been afraid the boy might try stowing away.

There was just time for a final checkout before they started, and Jim went over everything. It seemed to be all in order, down to the plastic bottles of liquid sealed with little nipples. No free liquid could be taken, since they'd be without apparent weight all the way.

Then he dropped to the pneumatic seat, while the other two buckled down beside him, facing through the plastic bubble that let them see. In the rockets from Earth, no windows were used, since the heat of the return might have ruined them. But here it was safe as long as they could cut off the glare of the sun.

They were on the opposite side of the Earth from their destination, traveling at the speed of the station — 15,840 miles an hour. To reach escape, they'd have to raise that to nearly 25,000. But there was no need for full-escape velocity here, since they only had to fight against Earth's pull to the so-called "neutral line" where the Moon's gravity would begin to overcome that of Earth. They would attain a top speed of only 19,500 miles an hour — only a little over a mile a second more than the speed of the station. Four-fifths of the work had already been done in getting the ship and fuel up the first thousand miles.

As the indicator reached zero, Jim cut on the blast, watching his accelerometer, and following the chart. The little ship began to pull away from its orbit behind the station.

There was no heavy thrust this time. It was like the trip to the relay station in that respect, and would require only a slightly higher top speed. They began to move out, still circling the Earth, but at a rising height.

Then they were another quarter of the way around, with their circular orbit straightening out toward their destination, and they began to rise more rapidly. Thirty-three minutes from takeoff they were nearly twenty thousand miles up. Jim cut the motors, and set back. From now on, there was nothing to do but drift, while the ship slowed under Earth's pull until finally it would barely crawl across to the pull of the Moon, to begin picking up speed again.

Pierotti looked up. "Very nice. And now we have nothing to do but talk. Well, I suppose I might as well turn in, since I sleep the first shift."

He went back to the sling that had to serve for all of them, one at a time, and was soon asleep, the straps that held him in moving slowly with his breathing. Charkejian sat at the port, staring out at space, like a small boy on his first train ride, while Jim began checking the orbit.

They were still within calling distance of the station, though the survey ship was equipped with only a small transmitter. They had sacrificed radio power for more oxygen for emergencies. Jim began calling, to be answered almost at once. It was Halpern's voice.

"You're doing fine, Jim," the colonel reported. "The observatory has been tracking you, and the calculations indicate you're right on course. Any messages?"

"Can't think of any," Jim told him. There was probably some fine and noble thing he should say to go down in the books, but he'd only left a few minutes before, and there was nothing to report.

"Okay, then. Good luck," Halpern wished him, and cut off.

Jim had drawn the second shift for the sling, and he turned in when Pierotti got up. He'd looked forward to this a long time, but now there was nothing to it. When they reached the Moon, it might be different, but until then sleep was as good an answer as any to killing time.

He woke to see Charkejian busy at the tiny electronic range, preparing the cans of food for them. With the solar batteries they carried on the hull, there was no lack of power for the range and the fans that had to keep moving the air, or for the air-conditioning apparatus.

Charkejian passed out the food, and then turned back to some discussion he'd been having with Pierotti, obviously still not ready for sleep.

"Sure, Chiam's an enigma to most of the world now," the scientist said. "He's only been in office for a short time, and there isn't much record to judge him on. But I knew him rather well when he was first taking up the study of rockets. He isn't at all like his uncle before him."

"I pray God you're right on that," Pierotti said fervently.

Charkejian nodded. "You should. Our former leader was a

savage at heart. He was loaded with national pride for outmoded things and hate for what he couldn't understand. I'm surprised the world didn't have worse trouble from him, and a lot of us were as worried as you were. But Peter's a realist. He'll be hard — he has to be. But he can face facts, and he can give in when he should. I think you'll find things a lot easier in the world from now on."

"Maybe," Pierotti agreed. "It had to come sooner or later. Your Combine can't hold back; it opened itself to progress when it taught all the people to read. Once they can get knowledge, they're bound to begin thinking for themselves."

"They'll have to. With colonies on the Moon, there won't be time for some of the old superstition and ignorance."

When Charkejian had gone off to sleep, Jim turned to the young Swiss. "Do many of the Combine talk like that?" he asked.

Pierotti shook his head. "Unfortunately not. Nor of any group. Charkejian's patriotic enough, but he can see the faults of his land, and he'd rather have them corrected. There are too many who think patriotism means only a blind acceptance of all the old prejudices. But I guess you'd have to say Charkejian is a scientist first of all. It makes him an internationalist, almost automatically."

Then he smiled. "But don't sell him short in estimating Peter Chiam. The fact that Chiam picked him might indicate that the young ruler is leaning in the same direction. Some of us hope so. If so, and with your President Andrews favoring better relations, some of the small countries may be able to breathe again, in spite of the stations."

They were already further out than man had ever been before, and their speed had fallen to a fraction of what it had been. The Earth was now only another moon to their eyes. Charkejian filled most of his time playing chess with whichever of the others was up. He was nearly an expert, and while he beat them, he seemed to get most of his pleasure from teaching them on the tiny board.

The halfway mark was long since past. Now the Moon was coming into view and growing. Jim re-checked his calculations, but he could find nothing wrong with them. At the start of the fourth day, their speed was down to 800 miles an hour, and they seemed to stand still in space.

At about 24,000 miles from the Moon's orbit, they began to reach beyond the Earth's sphere of influence, and the Moon's gravity began to draw them, speeding them up again. They could now see the details more clearly than most telescopic views from Earth. Without atmosphere, the Moon stood out harshly against space. The big craters, the so-called seas, and the strange straight rays were all visible.

Then it became harder to watch without a feeling of vertigo as the ship neared the big satellite. Jim cut on the cameras, guiding them from the instrument board. They seemed doomed to almost instant death on the harsh landscape below them, but he fought down the instinctive fear.

They were approaching the forward side of the Moon. The distance dropped sharply, while the big orb filled all their view. Pierotti wiped nervous perspiration from his face, but Charkejian sat staring at it as if he were coming home after a life of exile.

They sped by the Moon then, letting it pass between them and Earth. Its pull had distorted their orbit, but not enough to capture them or prevent their falling back to the station. A few minutes later they began to slip back from the top of their ascent and to begin passing by the Moon again. It rushed away to the side as they headed back toward Earth.

Jim had finally seen the other side of the Moon, about which so much had been speculated. The three men were the first ever to do so, since the satellite always turned the same face toward Earth.

But there had been nothing unusual to see, so far as he had observed. "It looks the same on both sides," he muttered.

Charkejian grinned at him. "To you, I suppose so. But to me, no. There was one mountain range there that was fantastic — it must be the highest spot on the Moon. And some of those craters! It's a whole new territory to map and explore, Jim. And I want to be one of the men to do it."

Jim could agree with that. Mapping was outside his knowledge, but more than ever he wanted to set foot on the pitted, meteor-cratered surface they had passed so closely.

Chapter 11 - Orbit's End

JIM'S figures showed that they were on a slightly different course on the return, but all of space looked alike, and it might as well have been the same one. With the high point of the trip finished, there was nothing to look forward to. Of course, there were the photographic films, already developed in the cameras. But these were locked, and couldn't be opened until they got back.

Until the last few minutes of their return, there would be nothing to do but talk and play chess with Charkejian. They were all getting bored now, the scientist last of all, and Jim was beginning to look forward to a change in their diet and a chance to take some kind of bath.

The air was good enough, but too many passages through the conditioning machinery had given it a chemical smell that was now mixed with the odor of their own bodies, too closely confined.

Living in such cramped quarters would have been hard at best, but the crude comforts here were far from the best. Jim supposed they were all going through a slight case of cabin fever. Various habits of the others began to get on his nerves a trifle, and he noticed them flinching at some of the things they saw him do.

There was another change. They had spent quite a bit of their conversational time discussing the possibility of setting up a colony on the Moon someday — one that could be built mostly underground, but with its own hydroponic gardens to grow food and maybe with a means to bake water and air from the rocks. In time, they had even considered, there might be a means of making rocket fuel on the Moon, which would cut down enormously on the difficulty of the trips.

It had grown to be a sort of accepted thing, and somehow they had begun to consider it an all-embracing project, belonging to all nations. Now, though, differences began to crop up. It was obvious that the sight of the Earth ahead of them was reminding them that it wasn't just a world of people, but also a world of separate nations, and of jealousies. Instead of "our" colonies, it began to be "your" colony, or "my" colony.

Jim found himself as guilty of that as the others.

In fact, Pierotti was least to blame. Probably because of the fact that he came from a small country, he simply called it *the* colony.

As soon as he could, Jim sent out a message toward the station, giving all the details he could remember. He wasn't sure that they could receive his call, but he hoped so. The sensitive receivers there might very well pick up his feeble signal. He got a sort of an answer, but his own receiver was too weak, and the words were lost in the general noise level.

They had long since left the pull of the Moon behind, and it was receding rapidly, far off to the side. Now they began to pick up speed at the same rate they had lost it before.

Some of the irritation vanished as they drew nearer the station. With the realization that they wouldn't have to put up with the discomforts much longer, they seemed somehow better able to take them. By the time they were within a day of the station, things seemed to flow back to a more normal level. They probably all felt a little foolish at some of their bad temper, but nobody mentioned it, realizing that they were all in the same situation.

At last they began the full rush down toward the landing. They were passing the Earth now, falling in a tighter and tighter curve as it pulled them harder, and approaching the orbit of the station.

Jim had been doing doubly cautious checking now, with Charkejian going over his figures. But he finally fell back on the radio.

Halpern's reply was nearly instant and greatly excited. "Congratulations! Congratulations to all of you — official ones, too, from just about every government there is. So far, you're being given the Croix de Guerre, or its equivalent, in every form made. Jim, they're even discussing a Congressional Medal of Honor. How's it feel?"

"Just plain tired," he admitted. "How'm I doing?"

"Couldn't be better. From what we can see, you won't have

more than a normal amount of correcting to do." Halpern apparently was rustling papers on his desk, and there were other voices in the background. "Nora says hi, and she'll see you later, Jim. Want me to read you any of the messages? We picked up your broadcast from the beginning of your descent pretty clearly, and I understand a tape of that is a best seller on Earth now. So maybe you'd prefer to hear a royalty statement."

Jim assumed Halpern was kidding about that. He couldn't claim royalties on a news broadcast, so far as he knew. But he was glad to hear of the interest it had aroused. Now, however, he had other business. "I'm beginning to brake," he said. "Want to talk to the others?"

At the answer, he handed the phones to Pierotti. There was still half a minute before he had to begin blasting, and he'd already made the corrections to the tilt of the ship. He waited, then signaled that blast would begin, while they buckled down.

After ten days, even the light pull seemed like a leaden weight at first as the rockets went on. He saw the other two, sharing the microphone, wince. Some of the energy from the tubes always managed to stir up a trace of static. It must have blasted into their ears. But as they drew nearer and the strength of the incoming signal increased, it wouldn't bother them.

He heard an exultant shout from Charkejian. "You hear that, Jim? I'm now entitled to top honors at home! And that means I'm free from taxes for the rest of my life!"

Jim smiled, realizing how much that could mean. Scientists seldom drew large salaries, and the Combine had a stiff tax rate that must have cost the man a lot of the books he'd probably needed.

Then Jim began working in earnest. They were nearly where they were supposed to be, but inevitably there had been trifling errors in the amount of pull the Moon had exerted and in other factors. The prefigured course was only an approximation now, and he had no time to calculate a new one precisely. He could have used the calculations he'd gone over with Charkejian, and then corrected any tiny differences with a final blast; but he wasn't too sure of the amount of fuel left. Anyhow, it would look better if he could bring the ship to a perfect stop, and he'd learned to do it with the ferry and taxi, so it should be possible.

It meant using the sense of feel, but he had come to rely on that. Now he began regulating the blast and working the gyroscopes carefully. They were rushing down at the top speed of over 19,000 miles an hour, almost a mile a second faster than the station, but beginning to slow as the rocket fought against the speed. They were curving in close to the Earth, aiming to land at the same spot where they'd taken off.

It felt right to him, and his observations fitted with what he expected. He began to relax, leaving the controls as they were. He could hear Pierotti saying something to the station about how relaxed he looked, and it sounded good to him.

Then abruptly Pierotti began shouting into the phones. He jiggled the controls of the radio and shouted again. "Dead!" he explained. Then he hesitated. "No, we're getting the carrier wave still. But nobody is talking. Maybe they've pulled out their mike plug."

"I heard somebody yelling something, and some sort of a scramble just before the radio went off," Charkejian said. He scowled at the silent phone. "It looks like trouble."

Jim stared at his rear screen, where the station was barely visible, but he could see no evidence of whatever trouble it might be. An attack from the other station? A meteorite hitting and rupturing the hull? There was no sign, and it didn't make sense. Besides, if the carrier wave was still hissing out, the power must still be on down there.

Pierotti began trying again, while Charkejian studied the rear screen and then forced himself up until his head was almost against the plastic observation bubble, where he could get a view of most of the Earth beneath the station.

Then Jim gasped and pointed. The station was near enough to be visible now, and beyond it, heading away from it, there was the streak of a rocket moving outward! He stole a hasty glance toward the charts, but he already knew no ferry would be taking off from here for the relay station now, and the trail he saw wasn't heading toward Earth. It looked almost like the orbit he had taken to reach the Moon!

He jerked his eyes toward the radar screen, but the three pips that showed the Moon ships indicated none of them had taken off.

Then he was forced back to his navigating. But Charkejian must have had the same idea. He was figuring busily, and now looked up. "If I saw enough for calculations, it might be a shot for the Moon's orbit, on the opposite side from where we were. But this is the only ship that was ready. Besides, it's a foolish thought. The Moon won't be there at that part of its orbit until several days after they arrive!"

The same thought had been bothering Jim. If that had been a rocket going out, it would arrive ten days after they had left the Moon — and it took the satellite two weeks to move halfway around the Earth, into a line with the station's direction of rotation.

Someday, Jim thought, he was going to make a landing at the station with nothing but pleasant surprises waiting for him and nothing to worry about. But so far it hadn't happened to him.

They were losing speed now, and beginning to drift toward the station.

Abruptly Halpern's voice sounded in the phones, and Pierotti bent over so Jim could hear. "You still there?" the colonel asked dully.

"We're waiting," Pierotti answered.

"Okay. You're doing fine. Just come in as you are. And I'm sorry about the interruption. Nothing serious, I suppose. I'll explain when you get down." Then, softly but still audible, there was a faint groan and something that sounded like: "The darned fool. The poor darned fool kid!"

"Freddy!" Jim guessed as the radio went dead.

It could only be Freddy. Maybe the boy had decided to go out to meet them, expecting them to come in from the same side as they'd left — though he should have known better. Or maybe he was trying for greater things!

With only half of his mind on the landing, Jim had somehow managed to keep things steady. They were apparently going to set down into a permanent orbit behind the station, in almost the same spot as their original berth.

He waited, then cut the blast. For a moment, he sighted on

the station and the Moon ships, before beginning to unbuckle himself. "We're here," he announced. It had been a good job of piloting, he realized, and he should have been happy about it. But now the worry about Freddy had ruined it.

The other two reached for his hands, to shake them and to tell him how good everything had been, but he brushed them off. The taxi was on its way to pick them up.

Jim began removing the locked magazines from the cameras. Until those and all the instrument readings were turned in, he hadn't finished his job. The other two men began helping him. By the time the taxi had touched their lock, they were ready.

Nora was running the taxi, Jim saw. And even through the helmet, he could see tears in her eyes. This time he knew they weren't tears of relief at his return — there was no laughter mixed with them. She gripped his hand in welcome as he passed into the taxi.

He jerked off his helmet as she began pulling hers off when the lock closed. "Freddy?" he asked.

She nodded. "Freddy, of course. The fool! The stupid little fool! We were all waiting to get your first call, and paying no attention to him. So he grabbed the chance to take off. He's going to the Moon — in the relay ferry!"

Then she buried her head in her hands and began to cry. It was obvious that somebody at the station had realized that Freddy was on no course to connect with his destination.

Jim pushed her gently to the far side of the seat and took the controls, heading back toward the station. He had to turn in his log and the other data to Halpern. It wasn't something that he relished now, but it had to be done.

"How much fuel did he take?" he asked her.

If there had not been enough, it might work out all right. Freddy would then miss the speed needed to carry him too far, and would go into a long narrow ellipse that would simply bring him back to the neighborhood of the station, and then Jim could go out in one of the ships and pick him up; it would be difficult, but it might work. With more fuel, however, the elliptical orbit might be too long — and returning would be no good if the oxygen ran out first.

Nora shook her head faintly. "We don't know exactly. At least two of the smaller tanks from the Moon ships. Terry spotted him taking off, and saw them fastened to the ferry. But it was too late to stop him."

And too late to do anything, Jim realized. With that amount of fuel, Freddy might or might not have been able to land on the Moon, if he'd started right. But it would certainly be sufficient to give him speed enough to get to the Moon's orbit and beyond. There wasn't any use planning a rescue now!

Chapter 12 - Futility

THERE WAS NO celebration at the station of the return from the Moon. One had been planned, but nobody could have gone through with it. Even those who hadn't liked Freddy were shocked, and they could feel what Colonel Halpern was going through.

Jim took the reports and films in to him. Halpern sat alone in his tiny office, with his dry grief held down under a hard will. He took the reports and films from Jim with no show of emotion, however, and signed the log of the voyage. "Thank you, Pilot," he said officially. "Well done! You are now relieved of your command!"

Jim hesitated, and then went out without mentioning Freddy. Behind him, Halpern sat stiffly, working woodenly at the papers on his desk.

Jim heard the few details that could be learned from the others. Freddy had kept mumbling about getting possession of the Moon before foreign spies claimed it, but nobody had paid much attention. The boy had seemed to be busy enough with his new duties as ferry pilot. And since he now had the job officially, nobody was surprised when he began requisitioning supplies for the ferry. He used forms signed by his father, apparently, and the forgeries on them were clever enough to have fooled any but a trained expert. He'd dropped hints that he had to make a trip up to the relay station for some emergency work to be done, and nobody had questioned it.

He'd also pilfered the supply dumps for some of the things he had needed. Men checking the supplies were coming in now to report that there were tanks of oxygen and stores of food missing. Unfortunately, nobody could be sure of the exact amounts missing. In the hurry of building the Moon ships, it was easy to miss one or two tanks normally, or to have some supplies scattered about where only a complete inventory would turn them up.

Just how Freddy had managed to get the two big tanks of hydrazine and acid was another mystery. He had used the taxi frequently, and must have lugged them over by using that, counting on the excitement of the survey return to cover up for him.

"Could he have hooked them up to work?" Nora asked.

Jim thought it over and nodded. The same valves could be used, since they were standard up here, and would screw into the fittings designed to permit refueling the ferry. He must have prepared his fastenings in advance and then done the actual coupling at the last minute. He'd been all ready, and it was only by an accident that Terry had seen him taking off. Halpern had found a note in his quarters, simply saying that Freddy had taken off for the Moon, and not to worry because he had it all figured out.

Jim's microviewer and films were missing. Freddy must have taken them along for reference material. The astronomers were still tracking him, and word came from the doghouse that his ship had reached a slightly higher speed than Jim had used. Freddy's ship would pass the orbit of the Moon before it began drifting back. The latest figures on his speed and distance were posted on the bulletin board outside the commissary, and Jim copied them down before wandering inside. He was at loose ends, as most of the staff seemed to be. The dining hall was crowded with people who had apparently wandered in for coffee and news, and now just sat. It was unusually quiet.

Charkejian motioned to a vacant seat, and Jim dropped down beside him, studying the figures. The astrophysicist leaned over to examine them, and began calculating the orbit. Jim had meant to do the same, but the scientist was faster at it.

Abruptly, Charkejian grunted in sudden excitement. "You figure it, Jim, while I recheck this. Unless I'm crazy . . ."

At first the course meant nothing to Jim. Then he began to see what the other meant. A measure of excitement crept back as his pen scratched out the course. At Freddy's speed, he would cover the early part of the trip in less time. But there would be no Moon waiting as he neared what should be the place where the satellite's gravity would take over. Instead of speeding up in a rush toward the Moon, the ship would go on slowing under the feeble pull of Earth. It would pass the Moon's orbit and begin an equally slow fall back toward its starting point. But days would pass at its slowest speed.

"Well?" Charkejian asked. He glanced at Jim's figures, compared them to his own, and nodded. Abruptly, he was on his feet, heading toward Halpern's office.

"But the men in the observatory should have known this, if we're right!" Jim protested.

"They've got too much work in the doghouse just keeping him tracked at that distance to have time to think yet," Charkejian answered. And knowing the job it must entail, Jim had to agree it was probably true.

Yet for a second Jim stood there, torn between the excitement of the facts the course had revealed and the fear of arousing any hopes in Halpern before they could be sure. He stared again at the course he'd charted, and then was suddenly sure. Charkejian was already down the hall, but he slowed at Jim's shout, and waited until they were together again.

Halpern should have retired to his private quarters, but there was still a light in his office. Jim knocked quickly, and then threw the door open before he could get an answer, to see the colonel lifting his head from his arms.

"He can make it, sir!" Jim shouted at him. "Freddy can reach the Moon!"

Halpern shook his head thickly, while the anguish on his face melted into the expressionless calm Jim had seen before. He stared at them until the words registered in his mind. Then he shook his head again, and there was no hope in his voice. "How? There's no skyhook up there for him to hang onto while he waits, Jim. Even I know more about space navigation than that. I don't need any false comfort!" Jim dragged out the paper with his figures and put it down in front of the colonel. "Look!" He pointed out the course with his finger as the older man stared at it. "Freddy's built up enough speed to carry him out here, as I figure it. He won't have any help from the Moon, but he will still pass beyond its orbit. Then Earth's gravity will lick him, bring him to a stop, and start him back — he hasn't hit escape velocity, so he has to fall back. The important thing is the time, though. This last little section of his orbit will be so slow that days will pass. Four days, to be exact!"

Abruptly Halpern focused his eyes on the paper, frowning as

he began to catch the idea. "All right. Go on," he prodded.

"The point is that instead of five days just to reach the Moon's path, Freddy is going to take nine days to fall back to it! And by then the Moon *will* be there!" Jim hesitated, and then summed it up. "Your son didn't make a mistake as we thought. He knew he'd never have a chance to take off at the right time for the five-day trip, so he planned to use the only opportunity he had. He figured on a nine-day course. And he was right. It will work."

Halpern lifted his eyes to Charkejian, who pulled out his own figures and passed them over. "It checks," the scientist said. "Any errors will be small enough for him to compensate for with a minimum blast on landing." The colonel nodded at last. His face had lost some of its coldness, but the hope that Jim had expected didn't appear. He smiled at them wearily, folded the papers and handed them back.

"Thank you, gentlemen," he said. "I'm glad you came to me with this. It will help to know that Freddy wasn't the crazy fool we thought he was in all ways. At least he didn't forget everything you'd taught him. I guess he was better at mathematics than I thought. I can be proud of that." He sighed, then shook his head slowly. "But it doesn't change things much. I suppose I'd rather have him reach the Moon before he dies — it seems better, somehow. But this won't save him."

"We can try a rescue. I'm volunteering for the trip," Jim offered.

"With what?"

The question seemed to cut the rising optimism away from Jim, leaving him with no answer. The little survey ship had never been designed to land on the surface. It might be re-equipped, but that would take time and supplies they didn't have. It wouldn't even be safe for another survey course around the Moon without long tests for strains from the acceleration it had taken. It had been designed for the one purpose, to be broken up after the trip, and even adding more fuel tanks and increasing the motor size for landing would be a nearly impossible job in the time they had.

To do any good, the rescue ship would have to leave in four days. It wouldn't be a real rescue, even then; all they could do was to carry supplies to last until the main trip could be made. There was no sense in dreaming about landing and taking off from the Moon again, since it couldn't be done. All that they could hope for was to get oxygen and food to Freddy to keep him alive — if he landed safely — until the big ships could arrive. And they wouldn't be ready for quite a while yet, in spite of the excellent progress that had been made.

The survey ship obviously couldn't be ready within the four-day deadline. Yet if they missed that, the Moon wouldn't be in a position they could reach until another two weeks had passed. That would mean a total of twenty-three days, counting time for the trip, before Freddy could be reached. It seemed improbable that he had taken enough supplies to last that long.

Still, something had to be done.

"There's the other ferry," Jim suggested finally. "We might try doing what Freddy did. With a more economical course, we could carry more supplies."

Halpern thought it over briefly, and then shook his head.

"I appreciate this, Jim," he said. "But I flatly forbid it. Don't think I wouldn't like to see it done. After all, he's my son. But I can't permit any hairbrained rescue that will only put another man's life in danger. All we can do is to hope that some miracle will come along to let him last until the regular trip — if he even manages to land. But thanks, anyhow."

He meant it for dismissal, but Jim couldn't leave until he was sure everything had been covered. His mind was reaching for anything that might offer some chance. Even if a scheme didn't work, it would sometimes suggest other possibilities.

Halpern seemed to read his mind this time. "If you're thinking of the robot brain that was supposed to pilot the ship, I've been considering it. But it won't work."

"Why not?" Jim asked. "It would save us the need of checking the ship — we could take a chance on trouble in a case like this when no life is involved. What have we got to lose?"

"We don't have anything to gain. The computer isn't able to handle anything as tricky as a landing." Charkejian sighed. "It wouldn't be. Even with it controlled from here, it wouldn't work,

Jim. There's about three seconds delay from the time it could send information back until our signals reached it again. And that is too slow for landing maneuvers."

Jim had known that radar, traveling at the speed of light, still took a second and a half to reach the Moon, but he had forgotten it for the moment; men still weren't used to the distances involved. But it would make any remote-controlled landing impossible, he saw.

Halpern picked up the papers in an automatic attempt to bury his feelings in the routine of his work. "You might spread the word that Freddy will reach the Moon; it should make some of our people feel better," he said.

This time there was nothing to do but to leave. Jim let Charkejian go to spread the word about Freddy's course, while he turned toward Jonas' office. The supervisor wasn't there, since he'd been called down to Earth and wouldn't be back until the next rocket up. But the big charts on his wall were what Jim wanted to see. He studied them, but they contained no new information, as he'd hoped they might. Finally he swung away and went looking for Thorndyke.

The announcement of Freddy's course was just being given over the loudspeakers when Jim found the foreman. For a moment, the man's face lost some of its look of gloom, but it came back as Jim summarized his conversation with Halpern. Thorndyke had probably been the hardest hit of any of them by Freddy's plight.

"So it means nothing," Thorndyke said when Jim finished. "The boy can't hold out until the main trip!"

"When will that be?" Jim asked. It was the information he had come to get.

The engineer grimaced. "It's supposed to be about four weeks before we finish, and a couple more weeks before they take off. I suppose we can skip the waiting period for tests and things, but . . ."

Three weeks! Then they would have to wait until the Moon was in the right position. That would make it a minimum of thirty-two days before takeoff, and five more days to get to the Moon.

They couldn't wait that long. But apparently there was nothing else they could do!

Chapter 13 - Last Hope

JONAS arrived that night on the rocket, but he went to his sleeping quarters at once, and Jim had to wait until the next morning to see him. Properly speaking, of course, there was no night or morning on the station, but they kept the same time system as that on Johnston Island, and the old terms remained in use. In Jim's mind, it was the eighth day before Freddy would land on the Moon.

He had to wait in the outer office while Jonas and Halpern conferred. But the time wasn't entirely wasted. To Jim's surprise, there had been a whole reel of microfilm correspondence for him — and that included only what the office at the Island had considered important. He skimmed most of it, amazed at some of the offers.

Apparently he would collect royalties on his broadcast from near the Moon. The tape company could have used it without payment, but had signed him to a standard contract — needing only his signature; they frankly admitted such treatment of him was worth it for good publicity. There was an offer for his name on a ghostwritten book about the trip, and numerous other business. He stared at them, realizing he could be rich overnight.

Halpern left then, and Jonas called Jim in. The supervisor glanced at the reel of tape and nodded. "Let our legal staff accept those offers for you, Jim. They can handle it all. We can use the publicity, and the money may be a good thing, even if you don't really need it. Okay?"

It didn't mean much to Jim, at the moment. He shrugged, passed the correspondence over, and signed the power of attorney form Jonas had already prepared for him. Then he dismissed it as he turned to what was important. "Mr. Jonas, we can't let Freddy die on the Moon. We've got to do something and do it fast! He can't wait five weeks for the scheduled trip in the big ships, even if he lands and has all the supplies he can carry!"

"Nobody's arguing about that," Jonas agreed. "What do you want?"

"I want to see the ships finished in time for the takeoff seventeen days from now. It's the last chance we have. Maybe Freddy can't hold out for three weeks, but we have to try it. And we can do it! I know we can, sir!"

"I've been thinking about it," Jonas said seriously, to Jim's surprise. "But I can't ask the men to drive themselves at that speed and force them to all the overtime we'd need. It has to be voluntary. Are you willing to take over full responsibility?"

"You tried making me foreman. I failed," Jim reminded him.

"You didn't fail when there was the pressure for finishing the station," Jonas said. "Besides, I don't mean as foreman — Terry, Dan and Thorndyke are doing all right for that. I mean someone who'll take over the whole thing and keep the men whipped up to a fever pitch. Get them to feel it can be done. A lot of them will remember what you did on the station and follow you in an emergency. Well?"

"Call them together," Jim told him. He didn't care whether he was head of the men or merely an errand boy, as long as the work was done. It was an entirely different feeling from what he'd had as foreman; he was counting on the men, not on himself. And maybe that was the element that had been lacking before.

Jonas turned the meeting of the crews over to him, and Jim put it to them simply and directly, outlining the work to be done. Then he stood back as they voted on it. It was no surprise to him when the decision to try it was unanimous.

"Okay," he told them. "Let's go!"

Some of the newer men looked surprised at his taking over, but the three foremen and the others who had worked on the station accepted it without bothering to think of it. They gathered around him, adding their suggestions and whipping themselves up to the assurance the work would somehow be finished in time. Then they moved out to the ships, while Jim went for the taxi and began moving up materials for them.

He could see the progress made late that evening as he called off the first shift. The big ships were taking shape already.

Down on Earth, the papers were making a big splash of the effort to rescue Freddy. The flimsies that came up with the rockets were filled with it. They had given him up for lost, but now they were publicizing the fact that there was still a chance. Surely, they argued, if Freddy had been able to figure out the course he took, he must have realized that it would be more than three weeks before he could be saved. He would have taken enough supplies to last.

Jim could only hope it was true. From what they could check on, it seemed possible, but there was no certainty.

He learned that the pilots had all independently volunteered to try an immediate trip, including Gantry. But Halpern had turned them all down. By now, Jim was forced to agree with the colonel. The chance of succeeding was too small for the risk, and all the effort would be needed in rushing through the main trick. There would be work enough for the pilots in bringing up the supplies.

But Mark Emmett couldn't see it. He came looking for Jim and Nora while his ship was being unloaded.

"I don't need any special ship," he suggested to them. "I can make it to the Moon in the regular third stage. Yank out all excess weight and take only what I'll need to help Freddy. Cut off the wings, controls, and a lot of the atmospheric streamlining. Dump out the automatic pilot. Then load her to the gills. As she is, with about thirty tons of freight and all that other stuff, she's good for sixty-two hundred miles an hour speed change; she'd only need thirty-four hundred more to land on the Moon. It can be done, Jim. Without Halpern knowing."

"And I suppose you mean we're to help you? Maybe get some of the men here to pitch in on the sly?" Jim asked.

Mark grinned back at him. "I wouldn't exactly ask anyone to break orders. But if I just sort of found the ship cut up a bit, and stocked with fuel and supplies, I couldn't waste the chance, could I?"

"I could arrange it with Thorndyke," Nora said thoughtfully. "He hasn't taken Halpern's decision very well. And . . ."

Jim stared at her in surprise. "I thought I was supposed to be the rebel around here — the one who wouldn't co-operate! Nora, how many lectures did you give me about everyone working together, instead of trying to get things done alone? You and Jonas were good at that."

"You don't want Freddy to die, do you?" she shot at him. He grimaced. "Of course I don't. But, darn it, Halpern's right. This isn't a one-man trip. The government isn't building those three ships out there at a cost of half a billion dollars because they enjoy spending the money. They're doing it because it's the only way to get to the Moon safely. It won't do us a bit of good to have someone else dead or dying on the satellite before we can get there — and that's almost certainly what it would mean."

Nora grew more doubtful as he went on. Some of the words sounded strange in his mouth, and he knew they were ones he had borrowed from Jonas and even from Nora herself. But they made sense. This wasn't a case for a single hero. It had to be done with a full crew and ships designed for the job.

"Besides," he finished, "we can't afford such stunts now. We don't have the fuel to waste. It's going to take all we can get up here to have the ships fueled in time. And we can't spare the rocket or pilot from supply work. It won't work, Mark!"

Mark shrugged and then grinned in amusement. "I guess you've grown up, Jim," he said, but it was no compliment in his terms. "Congratulations! Very sound position. Your bosses would approve. And you'll make a fine master pilot when they get around to that position. Well, be seeing you."

He went off. Jim stared after him, wondering. Maybe he'd made some impression on the pilot, or maybe not. He saw Mark stop beside a group of the men who were eating and sit down with them, to begin laughing at something one of them said. Then Jim shrugged and went back to his own work. Apparently Mark had given up the idea. At least the pilot left on his regular trip back to Earth.

Nora sighed finally. "I guess I shouldn't have agreed with Mark," she decided. "But it's hard to turn down any chance."

They were putting the meteor bumper on the Moon ships now. It was a thin metal shielding over the inner nylon and plastic globe for the passengers, designed to soak up the shock of any meteorite big enough to cause damage, and the finishing touch to the passenger quarters.

There was a tremendous amount of wiring and connecting up the automatic machinery inside still, as well as general work.

Stocking the ships would be a separate big job, though some of that was going on already. But with the passenger shells completed, much of the work could be done faster, since men could work inside without their suits.

Jim was busy welding when Mark came up in the rocket again. Then he looked in surprise awhile later when Poorhouse's rocket also came up. Usually the trips were staggered more. He saw that Nora had finished the unloading of Mark's ship and was stacking parts at the dump. Jim looked for Thorndyke, but couldn't find him. He turned the work over to Bill and went out in the ferry ship, which could be used as a taxi when there was extra work. He had to begin unloading for Poorhouse so that the ship wouldn't be held up in its return.

He was vaguely surprised that Mark's ship was still there, though it probably meant some official business to transact. There was no sign of the pilot. Jim stared at the ship thoughtfully. Then he shrugged. For a moment he'd been suspicious, but he could see no sign of damage to it. The wings were still attached, and the streamlining was still in place.

He was kept busy on Poorhouse's ship then. He was glad to see that most of the cargo this time was fuel. The huge amounts needed for the trip were a major problem. Of the half billion the trip would cost, over fifty percent would go for fuel. It would take a fantastic quantity for the trip. If they had to, they might even be able to skimp on some of the other work and supplies, but the hydrazine and nitric acid were indispensable. Moving it was slower than Jim liked, too. He had to couple onto the big freight tank in the rocket and pump it out, then haul it across to one of the ship tanks and pump the fuel in. But at least it wasn't as bad as the hydrogen peroxide needed to drive the big ship pumps on the trip. That required special treatment to make sure it wasn't contaminated.

He was nearly through when he saw the stir near Marks ship. Men were suddenly pouring out of it in their space suits, shooting themselves back toward the Moon ships. Jim gasped as he saw the number who were moving from the rocket. No normal work on it could require such a crew, and nobody had been assigned to any repair work there, as far as he knew.

He let out a yell, completely useless in the confines of the ferry, as he realized he'd been tricked. He should have been more cautious. Today was the right time for the takeoff to the Moon — four days after Freddy had left — and the station was now in the right position. He should have been alert and used extra precautions. Now it was too late.

There was a blast of hot gasses from the motors of the rocket and then it began to move. At the first touch of acceleration, the wings and fins snapped off, and the larger part of the outer sheathing fell away. Men must have been busy cutting them loose for hours. Only enough had remained uncut to hold them together until the first strain.

The little radio in the ferry blinked a red light, and Jim threw the switch. Almost at once the laughing voice of Mark came from it. "So long, guys. See you on the Moon. Jim, you reading me?"

"I can hear you," Jim told him angrily.

"Okay, pal! Just don't blame Nora. We got her off the taxi on a rigged excuse. She didn't have a thing to do with supplying me."

Jim flipped the switch off without answering. The fool, he thought. With the big ships being rushed to completion and every single supply rocket needed to bring up fuel, Mark had to do this!

Then his anger cooled and he threw the switch back. "Mark?"

"Yeah?"

"Take it easy, at least. Don't try to land if you see Freddy is going to crack up. Go into an orbit as tight as you can around the Moon and we'll pick you up later."

"I'll think about it," Mark's voice told him. "And give my best regards to the colonel. Tell him he'd have done the same once, maybe. So long, spaceman!"

"Good luck, Mark!"

The radio went dead, and Jim stood watching the stripped-down rocket taking off for the Moon. It was already beginning to vanish from sight, except for the fire of its exhaust that stood out against the dull black of space.

He knew he had done the right thing by refusing to disobey orders and take such a chance. Yet somehow it hurt to realize that another man was doing it. Freddy had been Jim's responsibility, and he felt like a coward now as he watched Mark leave.

He wondered if this kind of growing up into a cooperative person was really worth the trouble.

Chapter 14 - Stress and Strain

FIVE DAYS LATER there was a break in the work. Great as the rush was, everyone knew that there was no use in trying to get anything done while the question of whether Freddy could land was decided out by the Moon.

The telescope in the doghouse had been focused carefully near Dewey Bay — the section which had originally been chosen as the best spot. It still looked like the best, after a careful study of the films Jim had brought back, but Freddy couldn't know that, of course. Still, he'd read enough to know it was the logical spot, and he had maps with him on the microfilms to enable him to find it.

One of the younger astronomers was broadcasting an account through the speakers in the station. Men were clustered around, sitting silently as they listened. Even Halpern had come out to join Nora and Jim, unable to stand the suspense in his office with no one to talk to. But now that he was out with them, he was sitting silently as the report came in.

Minutes went by, with nothing new. Then there was a sudden cry from the speaker. "Something's showing! That's it. There's a rocket blast, right where he should be. And another one! Wait a minute, we're increasing the power on the light magnifier now. Two blasts showing, all right. Anybody know how to tell which is Emmett and which is the boy?"

Jim found a phone and began jiggling it, until he had a connection to the doghouse. "Tell the man announcing that Mark's ship was stripped, but that Freddy's would look mostly white, if anything can be seen. The tanks were just given a coat of reflective paint."

Word must have been passed along. A second later, the young announcer paused, and then picked up the account again. "We think we can make out the white on one of them. It must be Freddy Halpern. It looks as if he might make it. Hard to measure speed at this angle, but he's close to holding his course. The other one is going a little smoother, so it must be Mark Emmett."

He groaned suddenly. "One blast failed — Emmett's! Or it was cut off. There's still some sign of the other. And now that is disappearing. It's gone!"

The report didn't tell much. In a few minutes, pictures taken through the camera at the observatory doghouse were sent over, but they told even less. Up here with perfect seeing and the highest magnification, it was still a strain to see anything the size of a ship. Only trained eyes could do it at all.

Still, they knew now that Freddy had plotted his course correctly. He'd reached the Moon — either safely or in a crackup. There was no way of telling. Apparently Mark had even less chance. It had sounded as if he'd run out of fuel. He might still have lived, of course. On the Moon, the gravity was only one-sixth that of Earth, and the emptied fuel tanks could have served as shock absorbers. But it didn't look good.

Jim stood up, just as Halpern rose to his feet. The colonel twisted his lips in a tired smile. "Don't say it, Jim. I know what everyone thinks, and I appreciate it. Just don't say it!"

He went back inside again, and Jim headed for the work, calling the others to follow him. There were only nine days left before their own takeoff must be made, and there was still a tremendous amount to be done, even with all the overtime that was being put in.

A little better reaction from Earth might have helped somewhat with the morale here, though. Down there, the wave of sympathy for Freddy had been whipped up by the papers until a thousand crazy schemes for rescue were being proposed each minute. Then it had begun to die, as the limit of people's sympathies was reached. And there were plenty of selfish interests ready to capitalize on it and to stir up other feelings.

It seemed that the World Congress had been turned into a sounding board for many of those interests. Hints gave place to outright accusations that the United States had either faked the trip or deliberately sent Freddy ahead, using him as an excuse for a wild rescue drive that would justify the attempt to take the Moon for national interests. There was a big movement started to halt all such trips until a complete investigation could be made by members of the Congress.

On the surface, the Combine was against the movement. But Jim noticed that it nearly always seemed to originate in one of the Combine's satellite states.

Things broke into a wild debate that came within a hairbreadth of resulting in an end to space travel, though the United States managed to work up a last-minute rally and turn off the pressure into a resolution that actually had no meaning.

"I suppose you're going to tell me Chiam isn't deliberately using all this to halt our trip until he can beat us?" Jim asked Charkejian.

The scientist shrugged. "I can't tell you anything. Of course he is trying to keep your nation from getting any exclusive hold on the Moon. I said he could be hard when he needed to be, and he'll fight tooth and nail for his own country, just as you would. His gratitude to you doesn't mean he can grant all political favors. But I don't think he wants to stop all space flight. He's always been as much in favor of that as your own President."

It probably didn't matter, since the attempt had failed, Jim decided. But then Jonas set him straight on that. He came back from a rush trip to Earth, looking wearier than ever. The government was growing sick of the whole space business, except for President Andrews. The planners of the trip still had a lot of friends, but they couldn't count on enough.

"One more incident of any kind," Jonas told Jim, "and they may cancel the whole thing. They're sure we are totally irresponsible and just wasting taxpayers' money. The fact that the two ships got through our hands proves it to a lot of people, even though we can't police every nook and cranny up here."

The big problem remained the fuel. With only three of the supply rockets now, it was going to be a close job getting enough up in time. Jim grumbled at Mark at times as he watched Gantry and the other two pilots overworking themselves and their ships. With a million gallons of fuel needed, three ships weren't enough — not to mention the extra gallons Mark had drained from them for his trip.

"Maybe it should have been done under World Congress

mandate," Pierotti suggested. He was still at the station and apparently meant to stay until somebody recalled him. He was working as hard as anyone, and the blisters on his hands proved it.

"Nonsense," Charkejian snorted. "Did such a mandate ever work? What can a world debating society do about running a space station?"

"It would be more than a debating society if it had the Moon or the station," Pierotti said. "With power, they'd turn into a real international government. Most of the men on the Congress are fine people — even your representatives!"

Charkejian laughed, without taking insult. Jim wondered how much either was right, but he had no way of knowing. The nations wanted power too much to give it up, even to a World Congress of their own election. People might want peace, but nobody could relinquish the power struggle long enough to have any hope of such permanent peace.

There were rumors that President Andrews and Peter Chiam were exchanging messages on the subject, but Jim no longer tried to keep up with it all. His job was to get the ships to the Moon. Beyond that, it was up to the mercy of God!

Jonas went down again, this time to appeal for faster handling of the fuel, and to attempt to speed up the assembling of another supply rocket. But he had little hope for success. Even though only a third stage was needed — the first and second had been dropped by Mark on the way up — it couldn't be finished in the few remaining days. There was only one week left.

"And we'd better make it then, even if we have little hope of saving Freddy and Mark," he told Jim. "Once we get there, people will accept it. But if we can't take off in time, they'll be sure all the stories they've heard are true. Besides, the Combine station is finished and they may be ready to start work on a Moon trip of their own. With all the authority in the hands of one man, they can move faster than we can."

When Jonas came back the next trip, Jim knew he had failed to speed things up. They would have to do with what they had. He saw a strange look on Jonas' face, but the man refused to discuss anything but his failure. "There are some odd things brewing in top

99

circles, Jim. But they won't help us get going any faster, and I can't discuss them," was all he would say.

Jim forgot it and turned back to the work. Actually, finishing in time wasn't completely hopeless, unless the pilots cracked up under the strain. They were barely waiting for inspection on their ships between trips. In the long run, that could be dangerous; but they were willing to take the risk for the few more days. There were a few extra pilots to spell them, but again they preferred to stick it out, feeling that less experienced men would take more time or waste fuel that was needed for the big jump.

Without accidents, the work might just be finished in time.

And naturally there had to be an accident. Bailey discovered the trouble on one of his rounds of inspection. Something had happened to one of the fuel tanks. Either it had been faulty and its weakness had finally shown up, or carelessness had injured it.

At any rate, it had sprung a leak, and the fuel inside was vaporizing and disappearing into space.

There was no way to see it easily, and it could have been that way for some time. The hole was small, and the big globe was as full-looking as ever, since the vapor pressure kept it inflated. But a careful inspection showed that a large portion of the fuel had boiled away. In space, at zero pressure, most liquids boiled at much lower temperatures than normal, and the heat of the sun helped. The bags and the whole ships were painted white to reflect the sunlight, but some got through, even when the black patches left for heating were not turned outward.

They managed to seal the hole and to run careful tests on all the other balloons. But by then the damage had been done.

Jim and Thorndyke checked each other on their calculations as Jonas and Halpern paced about, waiting for the decision. Finally Thorndyke shook his head. "Not a chance. No matter what we do, we can't refill that fuel tank and all the others that need it in time. The ships won't carry it up, and from what the Island reports, they don't have enough spare hydrazine. They weren't counting on another rush order."

"They should have counted on it," Jonas muttered. "In this business, nothing ever goes right. All right, can we take off with what we will have?"

Jim vetoed that. "We're not leaving that much margin. We had already decided we could shave ten percent off — and that leaves no room for further cuts."

Halpern gave up, looking sicker. He must have had some faint hopes until then, but now he buried them. "All right, if you can't you can't!"

"We'll still try to do it, anyway," Jonas told him. "We've got to try, until the last second."

"Maybe we could try something," Jim suggested suddenly. It was a wild idea he'd thought of idly before, but never taken seriously. "If we could save fuel on the return, it would make things possible. And if we cut into Earth's atmosphere — just barely touching it — to slow our speed until we'd rise up to the station about like a supply rocket again . . ."

"No!" Halpern vetoed it flatly. "Someday it might be done, and it would save a tremendous amount of fuel to use atmospheric braking on the landing. But these ships couldn't take enough temperature rise."

Jim knew it was a wild idea. There was only one thing left, and that seemed even wilder. He separated from the others and went down the hallway toward the scientific side of the station. He found Charkejian working over a group of delicately etched plates, studying them with a microscope and taking measurements. The scientist looked up as he entered.

"Can you get in touch with Chiam by radio — in a hurry?" Jim asked him.

Charkejian nodded, surprise on his face. "I suppose so. Colonel Halpern has been co-operative in the past. There's no rule against my calling, if I dictate a tape to give the colonel a few seconds advance to monitor it. I think my right to ambassadorial courtesy will cover it." He studied Jim thoughtfully, then asked, "Why?"

"Just tell Chiam I need all the hydrazine I can get — desperately! Tell him I'll be glad of any favor I did him, but only if I can get the fuel. Or don't the Combine rockets use hydrazine?"

Charkejian straightened, and his face was serious now. "They use hydrazine, of course. But Jim, I wouldn't count too much on this. If you asked for a fifty-carat diamond a week, you might get it. But this runs pretty close to asking him to help your country take over the Moon. He isn't going to wreck the Combine plans, no matter how grateful he is."

"He owes us some fuel," Jim said stubbornly. "We used a few tons on the trip to rescue him. At least he can send that much up to us."

"Okay." Charkejian laughed softly. "I'll tell him. But something tells me you'd never be much of a success in dealing with absolute rulers diplomatically, Jim."

Jim didn't care about that. If it got him even one extra gallon of fuel, it was worth the try. He wouldn't count on it, and he didn't like asking for it, knowing he'd probably be refused. But something had to be done, and he could think of nothing else.

Chapter 15 - Takeoff

TWO DAYS BEFORE the proposed takeoff, there was still a large gap left in their requirements. Jim had heard nothing from Chiam, and he wasn't surprised at that. The best figures they could work out indicated that the fuel they would have would leave them absolutely no margin of safety.

Jim had suggested taking the risk and hoping that they could manage to get guided missiles sent with fuel, piloted by automatic computers, in time. But it had been only a desperate thought, and he hadn't protested when Halpern told him flatly it couldn't be done.

Jim sat in his quarters now, angry at Freddy for having taken his films, which might have contained some hints. He could get other films, but it was too late now.

The copy of Oberth's book caught his attention, and he turned to it. Then he shrugged. It was a remarkable book for its time, but how could it help now?

He reached for it again, nevertheless. Anything was better than nothing. There was nothing there, however. And yet, now that he thought of it, he was sure the faint idea that was nibbling at the back of his mind had been in another book by the same man. Probably a later one. He tried to picture it. *The Road to Space Travel.* Something in that!

And then the title jiggled his memory. The idea sounded fantastic, and yet . . .

Halpern's aide stuck his head in. "Jim! Boss wants you on the double!"

Jim groaned, trying to fix his memory firmly as he followed. He found Halpern standing and staring at one of the portholes that had been installed in the office.

The colonel pointed out. "Jim, take a look at that!"

There were two rockets out there. And as Jim studied them, he could recognize the design from pictures he had seen as belonging to the Combine. "You mean that — that Chiam sent fuel?"

he asked.

"So the ships claim, or I think they do. They apparently didn't have time to find an interpreter. Here, Ernst!" He handed a microphone to Charkejian, who had come running in, still in his pajamas. "Find out if it's what we think it is."

Charkejian tried one language and then switched smoothly to another as he heard the answer. He listened, and then nodded.

"It's hydrazine," he said. "The last thing I expected. Will wonders never cease. Something big must be going on down on Earth if the leader will go that far. Want a translation, or just the idea?"

"Just the facts," Halpern said. "And make it quick, because I don't want anyone down on Earth spotting them and deciding it's an attack before I can send word."

Charkejian talked a minute more and turned back. "They have full loads of hydrazine. Sorry they have no more free ships. Can bring maybe four more loads before your takeoff time. Chiam regrets they can't send more. And don't worry, Colonel — apparently he was delayed while he squared it through channels. Your superiors know what the ships mean by now."

Jim went out with the ferry while Terry took the taxi. Either the Combine used the same type valves they did or had made sure the ships were fitted for the job. They began transferring the precious liquid. The Combine pilots had avoided getting too close until identified, but it made only a trifling difference in the time needed. The next ships could come in closer, anyhow.

Six loads, Jim thought. It sounded like a lot, and it represented close to two hundred tons of total freight. It sounded like a lot, and yet it was only a small quantity for the big tanks. But it might mean the difference between merely operating with a fractional margin and not having enough to make the trip.

He tried to express his gratitude to one of the pilots, but the man could only spread his space-suited hands and grin back.

When the transshipping was over, Jim found Jonas and Halpern busy assuring their headquarters that everything had gone right. Jonas lifted an inquiring eyebrow. "Well?"

"We're still going to be too tight," Jim answered. "But

there's another way to cut down on fuel. I read about it and then forgot it. I guess most people did, but it works theoretically and it might help." He drew out his pencil and began diagraming. "Instead of taking off directly for the Moon as we did before, we start with what looks like suicide! We head down directly for Earth, as if we meant to make an air landing there. We coast down, picking up speed, but not quite until we touch the atmosphere. Then, just as we start to swing around Earth, when we're about three hundred miles up, we blast out with as high an acceleration as we can stand."

"And that saves fuel?" Halpern asked doubtfully. "Looks as if it would take more. You can't get something for nothing."

"It isn't for nothing," Jim assured him. "It's based on the idea of getting back some of the work put into the job of bringing the fuel up. It's a thousand miles high now. By dropping back to a lower level, and then burning it up before we come back to this height — using its weight on the way down and not lifting it back — we have to recover the energy used to lift it in the first place. If we didn't it would violate all the laws of energy!"

"How much saving?" Halpern asked. "Wait a minute. I want this stuff computed." He handed the rough figures Jim gave him to the aide. "Take this down to plotting. Get them to run a first-approximation on it at once!"

Jonas was shaking his head, trying to understand, when the call came through. Halpern picked up the phone and listened. "How good are your figures, anyhow?" he finally asked. He nodded, and handed the phone to Jim.

The results weren't quite as good as Jim had hoped. They would lose fuel in their change of orbit to fall back to Earth. But it still came out to a slight gain in the amount of power they could get from the fuel. Added to the Combine contribution, it would give them a bare four percent margin over their absolute needs. Even with that, there wasn't much room for maneuvering, but it was a risk that could be taken.

Halpern was hard to convince, and Jonas harder. But at last they agreed, after a long conference with Gantry over the problem of piloting such a course.

"Thank God, the men for the trip have already been picked,"

Jonas said. "And since most of them are from up here, and the others have been brought up for some time, they're ready. You'll be pretty short-handed with most of your scientific talent gone, Colonel."

Halpern shrugged. Right now he'd probably be glad to have most of them out of his command.

Jim was no longer permitted to work the ferry. This time Perez insisted that the crewmen who were going would have to be in top physical condition. Gantry and Poorhouse, the other pilots, were brought up while replacements took over. Jim saw that Lee Yeng would be copilot for Gantry, and he was glad. The other was a stranger to him.

The rest and lack of work were probably good for them physically, and the men were winding up the tremendous job of finishing the ships on time. But Jim felt irritated and edgy watching others handle things. He saw the next pair of Combine ships come in, and then the final two. He'd written a formal note of thanks to Chiam, but it was still probably waiting clearance.

Surprisingly, now that the trip was about to start, the World Congress had little to say. There was a curious lull in their affairs, as if something were brewing, but no sign of what. They again put in a request for Pierotti to go along, and President Andrews managed to agree before any objections could be raised. There was grumbling, but no real protest. The precedent had been set up on the survey ship. The United States had no cause to fear Pierotti's presence, anyhow. Jim was out early before takeoff time, with Nora beside him in her copilot's uniform. He went through the cargo ship, checking the stowage of supplies and the functioning of the machinery, while the little ferry was hauling the bigger ships around into the most favorable position. He had less men under his command than the other two pilots, but that didn't bother him. Ten would be enough in the passenger globe. He'd seen partial listings, but he could no longer remember who went with what ship.

Then the men began to file out — or rather, the men and women. Science had become more and more a field for both sexes, and space had never gotten started with any real discrimination. It was inevitable that a good share of the passengers should be women. Terry Rodriguez looked longingly at them as he ferried them out, but he'd made his decision to stick with the station, and he was making no last-minute request to change. He checked the list, assigning men to their proper ships.

The time was running shorter and shorter. Jim had counted the men roughly, but he couldn't be sure. He went to the radio to report. "I'm still short on my crew," he told Halpern. "Counting Nora and myself, there are only seven."

"The others are coming. There have been some last-second changes," Halpern told him.

Jim grunted. If they held things up now . . .

Pierotti came out, and with him Jonas. "We're going on your ship," Jonas announced. "Maybe because we know you best."

"We?" Jim asked. "Since when were you coming along, Mr. Jonas?"

The man laughed, and his face was suddenly almost youthful. "Since I persuaded President Andrews to appoint me as his personal observer on the trip. And don't think I didn't have a hard time to swing it." He grinned, and found himself a place to hold himself upright while the cargo ship was tugged around into position. "I started all this as business, Jim. Sometime along the line, you space boys converted me. I wanted to go."

It was good to have him, and Jim told him so. He'd learned to have a lot of respect for Jonas. "Zero in three minutes," he called to Halpern. "I'm still one shy."

"I know it." The colonel sounded frantic. "Keep your shirt on, Jim. There's an official tangle. Five minutes delay. You've got alternate courses to cover such situations."

Jim muttered in disgust and clicked off. This wasn't like the opening of a convention. It had to be based on careful timing. The Moon wasn't going to wait for them. But the officials couldn't seem to get it through their heads.

"Five minutes," he told Jonas. "And then, whether it's okay or not, I blast!"

Jonas shrugged. "You're in command, except for orders from Gantry, until we get there. I can't tell you what to do."

Jim could hear Gantry and Poorhouse calling the station, in the same threatening, pleading tones. He waited, while the clock ticked away four minutes, and then began strapping himself into his seat. "Takeoff positions," he called, making sure the radio was open.

Halpern's voice was ragged this time. "Postponed five more minutes. Urgent reasons of safety. Your passenger is on the way, Jim."

Jim cut the switch and glanced out. The taxi was more than a minute off. He reached for the controls, watching the hand of the chronometer. It hit the zero, and he started to bring both hands down on the blast lever.

Then he stopped, shaking his head. He reached for the radio again. "Okay, Stanley acknowledging delay. But this is final!"

"Final," Halpern confirmed. "Thanks, Jim."

Jim sat back, avoiding the amused eyes of Jonas. All right, so he didn't feel like being a rebel any longer. He couldn't, with the lives of the others as his responsibility now. So long as there was any chance that there might be sound reason for the delay, he had to accept it.

The taxi bumped alongside, and Jonas worked the lock for the final time as Charkejian came in and hastened to his seat. He chuckled at Jim's surprise.

"In return for his assistance, Chiam gets a representative aboard again," he explained. "I didn't think I'd make it, but the acceptance came through in time. I didn't cause all that delay, though, Jim."

Co-operation, Jim thought. The officials of all countries were getting almost too thick with it. It must mean more than had been released.

Then the time ran out again. This time there were no more delays. Jim had the second revision of the course out in front of him, and most of it was already memorized. He called out the warning and began counting backward. Over the radio there was a confirming count, which broke off at zero minus thirty while Halpern wished them good luck, and then began again.

The chronometer hand met the indicator and Jim's fingers eased back on the lever. More than four thousand tons of ship and cargo stirred gently and began to move.

This time, Jim realized, he wasn't a mere replacement. There would be no Gantry sitting beside him to help if he should foul up the trip. Here was one case where nobody had more experience than he had, since no such trip had ever been made, unless it was by Freddy and Mark Emmett.

It would be the first real landing on the surface of a world without the help of an atmosphere.

For a second, the mixture of thrill and fear ran through him. Then he turned to the job ahead, figuring their course in his mind and body as he checked it with the instruments. Finally, he eased back on the control and the first blast cut off.

They were dropping toward Earth.

Chapter 16 - Holed

IT REQUIRED close estimating as they drew nearer the Earth. At the speed of over eighteen thousand miles an hour they would reach, and with ships having no streamlining, even a few wisps of air could cost them more speed than the maneuver would gain — if it didn't burn them to cinders! These weren't ships designed for atmospheric travel. But the closer they could get, the better it would be for speed. They had finally decided on a height of 320 miles.

Jim watched the long-range altimeter carefully, trying to make sure that he was within the normal variation. They came down now, and began to turn under Earth's pull. The interconnecting radios were open and the ships were holding in a compact group of three. It wouldn't do to spread, if they hoped to achieve the same course without costly maneuverings. Gantry was running the official count now. But he couldn't control all the blasts. That had to be done on each ship. He suddenly made up his mind. "Now!" The blast ripped out behind Jim's ship as he hit the lever. He checked the course and kept his eye on the screen that showed the others. He was almost precisely keeping up with Gantry, and Poorhouse was close enough. Gantry's ship, the *Hohmann,* would be the pace setter, of course. Poorhouse was at the left in the *Oherih,* and Jim to the right in the *Goddard.*

The acceleration wasn't as heavy as that of one of the supply rockets, but it was more than the Moon ships had originally been designed to take. They had to burn their fuel now as quickly as they could to throw off its weight here where they were close to Earth, rather than doing the work of carrying it higher again before using it. It was pouring out through the great banks of rocket motors in rivers, draining the big globular side tanks in a matter of minutes.

Jim was only barely conscious of the pressing weight that was crushing him. His fingers were leaden on the control board, but his attention was riveted on his instruments and the other ships. The

110

acceleration wasn't great enough to bother his vision.

They were rising again, around the Earth and arcing back up toward the station orbit. But now their speed was rising above that of the fall.

Gantry had the hardest job — it was up to him to decide when they were ready to cut blast His count began, just as Jim tensed to expect it. They were in smooth synchronization with each other.

All feeling of weight disappeared as the blasts cut off. He studied the other ships, wondering if there would be a slow drifting apart to mark errors in their courses. But he could see none.

From the station, a signal came out. "Perfect within our observation!"

It couldn't have been more welcome news. Jim heard Gantry's sigh through the speaker, and then the click of the switch being closed. The older pilot had the heavy responsibility, and Jim was glad of it.

And then, as always when drifting in space, there was nothing to do. The passengers unfastened themselves. Jonas, Pierotti, Charkejian, Nora and himself were nearly as at home in such conditions as they were on the surface of a planet. But he wondered about the others. He'd have appreciated having a few plain crewmen or maintenance engineers, but somehow he'd drawn five of the scientists. Probably Charkejian and the others had replaced his crew. It was the sort of foulup that could happen at the last minute.

He checked over everything, making sure it had stood the strain of acceleration, and was finally satisfied. Then he turned to Pierotti. "Want to help me release the balloons?"

The young man grinned back at him and began getting into a space suit. The release could have waited until near the end of the trip, but Jim felt more comfortable doing it at once.

They pumped the air out of the lock and climbed out through it into a forest of girders and onto the top of the cargo tank. At thousands of miles an hour, there was no feeling of speed. Only a change in rate or the resistance of air could produce that. They had the same momentum as the ship, and it was like standing on a still platform.

Jim grabbed a thin rope and tied it about himself, in case of an accidental slip or movement that might throw him off. But it was only a casual precaution. Pierotti seemed no more concerned as he followed Jim out toward the places where the girders holding the big balloons were fastened to the rest of the frame. They moved along from handhold to handhold.

Jim saw men coming out of Gantry's ship to do the same, and then others moved from the *Oberth*. He felt some satisfaction in knowing he'd been the first, though he suspected all the decisions had been independent.

They pumped the little remaining fuel back into the other tanks. The pumps were actually thin rollers that squeezed the bags empty. Here there was no pressure outside to force the empty globe walls together; and when not under acceleration, the fuel might clump into a sphere anywhere inside the tanks, so no ordinary pump could work. Then they loosened the big hitches. Bracing themselves, they shoved the framework and bags away, where the assemblies would drift off slowly back and sideways. Eventually, they would crash on the Moon. It was wasteful, but less so than using the fuel needed to brake the extra weight down to the satellite. They repeated the same action on the other side, and then went back into the *Goddard*.

The first day wasn't so bad. The five new voyagers managed to take it for most of the time. But then the excitement wore thin and their fears mixed with whatever weakness they felt. They hadn't much space training, obviously, and life under the spin of the station wasn't the same thing.

There were grumblings and bickerings, particularly when they realized that there was only a single tiny rest-closet and that they would have to sleep in shifts. They'd been told all that, of course. But now they were feeling it, together with the fact that they were imprisoned in a small globe, thousands of miles from Earth, and without any fixed up or down. There was a quarrel between one man and woman who both had several degrees after their names about which one would have the seat nearer the pilot, until Jim settled it by sending them both to the back. There were complaints at the smell of the food in the small cabin.

It reached the worst when one girl became space sick. She'd

been quiet before, but now suddenly she couldn't control herself. Nora had to chase about frantically, cleaning up and setting fans to high speed to purify the air. The others turned on the girl.

Pierotti got up then and went swimming back through the air toward them. Jim realized why he had been chosen for the position of a diplomat as he watched Pierotti soothe the others and bring some order out of things. Mercifully, the girl recovered quickly and there was no recurrence.

Jonas moved up at Jim's beckoning, to slip into the seat behind. "Is this what they call adventure?" Jim wanted to know.

The older man smiled. "I suppose it is, Jim. I imagine all through history, every great event has been loaded with such preliminary bickerings and later troubles. At least, I seem to remember that Columbus ran into trouble at the court of Isabella; and he certainly had enough grief with the inadequate crew of unwilling sailors he got. They'll probably be all right later. They're just realizing they can't get out and walk back."

Jim nodded and tried to forget his own grievances. He finally got into a game of chess with Charkejian, while Jonas kibitzed. Then he watched as the two older men played, surprised to see that it became an entirely different game when both players were expert.

Again, it was discussion of a colony on the Moon that finally filled the time. With five scientists there, the speculation on what could be done was almost fantastic. Jim wondered how much of it could ever come true. More than seemed likely, he suspected. It had taken only this last century for men to move from the ground into the air and then out into space. Maybe in another century the Moon could be converted into the livable world these people were dreaming of. At any rate, it gave them something to think about.

Certainly, if fuel could be made there, trips would become relatively simple and cheap. With such fuel, the ferry would need little changing to handle the trip regularly.

Things had shaken down somewhat by the time the third day began. Jim pulled out one of the survey pictures of Dewey Bay and began studying it. Its official name was *Sinus Roris*, on the northern section of the Stormy Ocean — actually less of a sea than the Sahara Desert, of course. It lay well toward the North Pole of the Moon, where the sun would strike the surface at an angle, and where there wouldn't be the impossible daytime heat to be found at the Equator. On the photograph it was a great dark plain, flat enough for a good landing, but with areas that offered good shelter possibilities. They had no idea how much danger there might be from meteors there, but it could do no harm to play it safe.

Unfortunately, though, they couldn't pick the ideal landing site, as the original plan had been. They'd be forced to depend on where Freddy had landed, since they would need to get to him as quickly as possible.

Suddenly the radar bipped at him, blinking with tiny pinpoints of light. Charkejian let out a pleased chuckle.

"So I was right," he explained. "I thought there was evidence of a small meteorite swarm due here. You're seeing something that's pretty rare, actually. But that's why I insisted on having the trip held back as long as I could, to make sure it would be safe. They should just pass before we reach that section. A couple of big ones — big as a small car, see? Those are really rare ones. We got signs of them on the observatory micro-microwave radar, and . . ."

There was a sharp, intense splatting sound, followed by a brief scream of air, and something that might have been an explosion! It had come from the bottom of the passenger globe, and now there was a movement of the air toward that section.

One of the women screamed, and a man was sitting back with dawning fear on his face as Jim dived down the central pole. He saw that the automatic detectors had been released and were moving slowly toward the small hole — like little balloons drifting in the air currents.

He grabbed an emergency kit from the wall, yanked it open, and slapped a prepared patch over the hole where the air was escaping. The internal pressure held it tight, until the cement could seal it.

Then he turned. At first, it looked as if they had been lucky. He bent over to examine the damage more closely, however, and groaned.

The meteorite must have been as big as a small pea. It had obviously hit with force enough to drive it through the bumper, meant to offer enough resistance to vaporize the bit of rock before it had time to break through. Then it had driven in at such a speed that the air had acted as a solid, piling up ahead of it, and heating it almost instantly to a gas. That had been the explosion. The meteorite hadn't gone through anything but the wall, but the shock from its vaporizing had acted like a small bomb.

The chief damage had been done to the central tube, down which the wiring from the navigation controls ran, on their way toward the rocket motors. Some of the wires had been broken entirely, and the rest were twisted into a messy tangle, with insulation laid bare in spots. There would have been even more damage if he hadn't been drifting with no electricity flowing through the wires. He felt sick as Charkejian joined him, to be followed by Nora and Jonas.

"Maybe you should have gotten this trip postponed another five minutes," he said to the scientist. "Or maybe that radar stuff of yours wasn't too accurate."

"Not very," Charkejian admitted. "It's still brand-new methods, and amazing we get any reliable results. Anyhow, there's always a faint chance of being hit by one, though it's pretty slim. You're lucky you didn't hit the main part of that little swarm."

Jim nodded. The man was right. If he'd taken off on the original schedule or the next, in defiance of authority, there was a good chance he'd have been hit by more, and worse.

There was still trouble enough. "Any chance more will hit while we're down here?" he asked.

Charkejian spread his hands helplessly. "Who knows? There's always a chance. But the end of the swarm is past by now. Anyhow, there's nothing you can do about it, so you might as well stay."

Jim had finished his study of the wiring. He could probably have repaired it, given time. It would have meant ripping off more of the tubing, up to a height where he could trace the color codes on the insulation of the wires, before he could run replacements. He might be able to rob wire from something else, if the ship had no spares. Probably the directory list in his official papers would show wire somewhere.

But with what he knew of wiring and the mess this was in, there wouldn't be time to get it fixed before they were landing on the Moon. And he couldn't use the rockets for landing until it was fixed.

Naturally, it had to happen to his ship! There wasn't supposed to be one chance in a hundred of one that size hitting; most of the meteorites were dust particles or smaller. Probably the meteor bumper would show pits where some of those had hit before the trip was over. But out of all the billions of cubic miles of empty space, he'd had to arrive here at the same time as that lump of rock!

"So what do we do about it?" Jonas asked.

Jim grimaced. "We yell for help, I guess," he decided.

Chapter 17 - Emergency Repair

GANTRY listened in surprise. Obviously he hadn't known there was any trouble. No sound could carry across the vacuum, and the flash of the meteorite must have been too small to notice on the outside. The leader of the trip consulted briefly over his intercom and then grunted reassuringly.

"We're pretty well staffed here," he said. "One of the maintenance crew helped to lay out the original wiring. We have tools enough. It shouldn't take too long. The men will be right over."

Jim turned back to the nervous passengers. Pierotti and Nora had calmed them somewhat, but they wanted official word now. "We got hit," Jim told them truthfully. "But it was a small meteorite. The hole in the hull is patched, and men are coming over to fix some of the wiring that got tangled up."

If they thought he meant the wiring that gave them light, instead of the controls of the ship, he was happy to leave it that way. He wasn't going to lie to them — that would ruin everything if they ever discovered it — but the less they had to worry about, the better. He saw Jonas nod approvingly as he finished.

Gantry came over with the two crewmen. The airlock was at the bottom of the globe, and he saw the mess of the wiring as soon as he was inside. But he stepped back to let one of the crew look at it.

The man whistled as he studied it. "Really chewed things up, didn't it? I don't have all the colors of wire, so I can't code it again. But I reckon we can patch it. Ted, get up to locker seventeen there and pass down that wire. And insulation."

"You seem to know where every ship carries its spares," Jim said in surprise.

"All carry the same stuff in the same maintenance lockers," the man told him. "It's my business to know about that."

It sounded logical enough, but it was the first Jim had known of it. He'd have to study the directory more carefully in the future. He watched as the wire was passed down. On the deck overhead, the other passengers were spread out, their heads projecting over the hole. Only Nora was missing, and she must have been sitting at the controls. But with the work in progress, and the mechanic's obvious assurance, Jim saw no reason to chase anyone back. It would serve some useful purpose in relieving boredom.

There wasn't much to watch, though. The man stripped away the tubing with metal snips and plugged in a soldering torch. His fingers laid out the good parts of the cabling neatly and he began pulling off the insulation with a stripping tool. There was no fumbling or uncertainty as he located each coded strand and began connecting the ends with the black wire he was using.

The watchers got bored in time and went back to their discussion. But Jim stayed there, trying to learn what he could of the skill required. It wouldn't do any harm to know how to make his own repairs.

It was finished finally, and the mechanic nodded. "I guess she'll hold. With the alloys they use in these things to save weight, I'm not too crazy about doing all that soldering. But to fix it right, I'd have to build a whole new cable."

"But will it last long enough?" Jim asked.

The man shrugged. "I can't guarantee anything. Nobody can test it without using it. But it should do the trick. Want to sign this for me?"

Jim stared at the voucher book held out to him incredulously. Then he bent over, laughing. Gantry chuckled, too. "It looks silly, Jim, but there's logic to it. It isn't just bookkeeping. They need to know what went wrong, and why replacements were needed, for future trips."

It probably did make sense, but the idea of signing for a job out here, as he might have done back on Earth, still struck Jim as funny. It offered the comic relief the trip badly needed. After Gantry and the men had left, he repeated it to the others, and "Sign this" was good for half a day of jokes before they exhausted it.

Pierotti was serving as radioman, passing on the words from Earth. Here on the bigger ship, they had a set that could reach back from the Moon, and there was no loss of communication. There was a lot of routine encouragement, along with news from the World

Congress, which was busy on space travel again. This time there was a demand from the smaller nations that space be internationalized — made free to all, with no rights to colonization or exploitation belonging to any single nation, as in the case of the seas. It was an idea that had appeared before, though it seemed better organized this time.

Pierotti, Charkejian and Jonas were all excited about it, but Jim had large doubts. The attempt had failed before. The number of the smaller countries meant nothing against the power of the Combine and the United States. Why should a nation already in space give up what it had?

Of course, some lip service was already being paid to the idea, as shown by the presence of Pierotti and Charkejian. But they were still only observers, not accepted officially as part of the personnel. Maybe it wouldn't matter in the long run. The former colonies in the New World were nearly all free now, and colonies in space would probably also win independence. But that was far in the future. At the moment, Jim had enough things to face without worrying about what he couldn't control.

The fourth day gave them a fine view of the Moon. Jim had seen it before, but those who were making their first trip found it fascinating, particularly when Charkejian pointed out the spot where they would try to land.

It was at the beginning of the fifth day when Pierotti suddenly shouted and turned up the volume. Jim felt a shock go through him at the words coming over. The World Congress had internationalized space! The smaller nations had won. Space could belong to no nation, but would be free to all, under a special committee being set up. The amazing thing was that both the Combine and the United States had signed the agreement, demanding only a twenty-five thousand mile limit to protect the stations they owned.

Jim heard the others discussing it, while his own mind whirled. But he had to save thoughts on that for later. They had crossed the "line" by then, and were picking up speed toward the surface that was coming toward them, still off to the side.

They were still too far away to have any hope of spotting the

119

ships of Freddy or Mark, but he kept straining his eyes there. It seemed doubtful to him now that either could have lived. Men weren't supposed to get into space in such hasty, makeshift fashion. It was ridiculous, when there had been this whole carefully planned trip nearly ready. And even with all the plans, things could go wrong.

They'd lived long enough to reach the Moon. But that was the easiest part of it. Getting to the surface in ships not designed for the job was another matter.

He had Pierotti turn the antenna toward the Moon and try to put through a call, but it was too far to be sure the negative results meant anything. With these ultra-short waves, anything between them and the two ships down there could cut off the signal. Pierotti kept trying without answer.

Gantry called the other pilots, checking with them on their course. The errors had been small ones, but he had decided to correct them now, instead of waiting to make a combined correction and landing orbit. Jim suspected that it was to give him a chance to try out the repaired controls. He'd been wanting to do so, but hadn't thought it possible, since it might waste a trifle of their fuel and since they would be separated unless all acted together.

His hands were sticky as he prepared to follow the procedure the three pilots had finally agreed on. It would be fine to test the repairs — but what could he do if nothing worked? It would simply give him longer time in which to realize that the trip would end with a crash on the surface! Yet he had to know.

He waited for Gantry's count, and then touched the controls gingerly. They would operate only at the lowest power and for a minimum time — with only a single tube in the big rocket bank doing the work. The ships needed only a trifling correction.

Then he felt the faint pressure of acceleration and saw a bit more of the surface of the Moon through the observation window, to indicate the ship had moved.

"All clear now?" Gantry asked.

"Everything perfect," Jim answered.

But he wondered. All the test had showed was that a single tube had responded to his controls, and for a few seconds. For all he knew, others might fail on the trip down.

Then he grimaced at his fears. Actually, it had been a pretty fair test. If one were hooked up properly, it showed that the mechanic had known his business, and the chances of the others working would be excellent. It was no absolute guarantee, but it was promising.

Time crept along as the ship seemed to be running toward the surface. If the fall weren't checked, they would land at a speed of six thousand miles an hour — enough to crush them completely. On their present course there was no chance of missing contact and sailing on by. They would strike straight for Dewey Bay.

"Nervous?" Nora asked him.

He nodded. "I guess scared is a better word. I can think of more things that might go wrong in a minute now than I could in a whole day before. How about you?"

"Pretty bad. But at least I don't have the responsibility. I wonder what it's like with Gantry."

Jim grinned in spite of his worries. "I get a picture of him finding something wrong. He'd climb out on the front of the ship and get ready to bat the Moon out of his path. And maybe he'd do it, too!"

"It sounds like the hard way to me," she said, but she smiled a little at the idea.

"It would be the hard way. Gantry has always had to do things the hard way. But he does them. Sometimes I wish I were more like him."

She snorted softly. "You don't know yourself very well, then, Jim. You *are* like him. You may have some advantages he doesn't have, but you go at life the same way. I guess that's why you and he trust each other. You both fight for things you can't possibly get — and you both get them!"

It didn't fit the picture Jim had of himself. He'd run into a lot of good luck, and there'd been more than his share of help from others. Some luck had been bad, of course, but that had to be expected. Sometimes things had looked horrible, but there'd always been some solution.

He shook his head. It was a fine time to start worrying about what he was really like! "Would you do it all again, Jim?" Nora asked.

He realized then that she was only making conversation to kill the growing tension, and he was grateful for it. But he considered her question carefully. "Of course I would. I knew when I first wanted to go to rocket school that it wasn't the easiest or safest way to live. I heard enough about the early test pilots and what happened to them. What else would I do, though?"

"Nothing, I guess," she answered. "And you don't think you're exactly like Gantry! How do you think he'd answer that question?"

She had a point there, Jim saw. Gantry had no questions about whether he'd picked the right job. He knew. And so did Jim. It was right, even if the rockets wouldn't fire when he needed them. Somebody had to open up space, after all! The radio went on again, and Gantry was calling the figures that gave their course. "Three minutes," he said. "We still can't spot the other ships. We'll head for the central area and make correction to land as near anything we can spot as possible. The first man who sees a ship down there will take command at once and guide us all down. Okay?"

It was about the only system they could use now. They agreed, and Gantry hesitated. "Two minutes," he called.

Then Nora pointed. On the rear screen, near the southern section of Dewey Bay, there had been a brief glimpse of something white. She was cranking up the magnification, and it could only be the ferry ship Freddy had used. There was no way to tell what condition it was in. There wasn't even time to think.

"Stanley taking over," Jim said into the microphone. He was forcing his mind over the courses and corrections possible, scribbling marks on the course chart. "One minute . . . fifty seconds . . . forty seconds ...?

He'd hoped that Gantry would spot the ship. He hadn't wanted the job. It was bad enough to know that ten lives depended on his skill at something he had never done before. Now there were fifty. But he couldn't back out after their agreement.

". . . Seven . . . six . . . five . . . four . . . three . . . two . . . one. *Zero!*"

He had already called the first figures for the blast correction, and set them up on his board. At the final count, his hand hit the controls.

Chapter 18 - Lunar Landing

THE *GODDARD* REELED under the shock of sudden acceleration as the rockets blasted out. For a split second, Jim wondered if any were missing. Then he was sure all were working. He couldn't mistake the feel of sound tubes at work, fighting against their speed and the pull of the satellite only five hundred miles below them.

Even at full magnification, though, it was still too soon to locate the best landing site. He could remember the details of the photograph, but it had been too much territory to memorize fully. He'd have to pick the best spot on the way down, and then pray there was a place for all of them. In the last few hundred feet, it would be every man for himself, until they touched the surface.

At two hundred miles up, he could begin to see some detail. Nora touched the screen, pointing to a speck there. "Mark," she whispered. Jim nodded and went on correction course. They would have to find a level place, fairly free of any large debris; the three main legs of the ship, attached to the motor platform, were self-leveling to some extent on their spring mounts, but on really rough ground, they might hit potholes or touch the edge of a rock that would roll at the wrong time. If one of the ships ever tilted, it would be ruined. Even if the men inside survived, there would be no way of getting it upright again, or taking it up from the surface.

Mark's ship had apparently landed about three miles from that of the boy. It seemed to be in the middle of a rough, ragged section where no landing should have been made, with no obvious path between. The ideal spot for the rescue ships would be somewhere between, to increase the chance of reaching both ships. But that was impossible.

Jim had to decide which would come first, and to make up his mind immediately. There wasn't fuel enough for any fancy maneuvering or hovering. The two had both been fools, of course. But Freddy had been the cause of the trouble, and he'd had less reason to disobey orders. He'd also had his father to consider, while Mark hadn't involved anyone else in whatever might have happened to him.

Yet Jim had promised Halpern that he'd look after Freddy! Reluctantly, Jim set his course to bring him near the boy's ferry. It would leave the other ship even nearer, but separated from their site by a section of rocks that might be nearly impassable. That couldn't be helped. There had been no other choice possible.

Jim's eyes danced from the course figures to the viewing screen. The whole section looked worse than he liked, though it was still too early to be sure. A few miles further out, there was a nearly ideal place, from what could be seen, but it would put them hours further from the rescue.

They were equipped with a small tractor on the ship which could travel across the lunar landscape, powered by the breaking down of hydrogen peroxide without the need of air for its motor. But they were limited on fuel for it, and couldn't trust it on too long a trip until it had been tried in actual use. They had meant to bring two of them, but a lot of such details had been planned, and then had been dropped to save on weight and time in the final rush. As it was, they couldn't risk the one tractor in too long a rescue attempt.

The trip down seemed to be taking forever, though Jim knew that it would be no more than ten minutes from the first blast until they touched the surface. He was simply draining the most out of each second, his mind churning in all directions at once, and still managing to stick to the basic business of setting their course.

So far, maneuvers had been familiar enough. It wouldn't be too strange until the last few minutes. The tough part would be the judging of the blast to kill the final bit of their speed exactly as they came in contact with the surface. There was a feeler "leg" in the middle of the rockets, designed to solve that problem; within reason, if they came down too fast, it would be jarred up and turn on full blast to kill their speed; if they slowed too much, it would help somewhat in the following drop. And in any event, once they were fully down, it would cut off all rocket power instantly. But it was a fine way to waste fuel, hovering up and down. This had to be done right.

They were only about a hundred miles up now, slowing satisfactorily. Details began to appear on the screen. Jim blinked his eyes, catching a quick glimpse of the other big ships beside him. Then he looked back at the screen. The slight rest had helped his vision. He could begin to make out the lay of the land now.

He saw that it was a good thing he hadn't picked a site near Mark's ship. The little dot on the screen was in the middle of what seemed to be knife-sharp hills and pitted valleys. It was inconceivable that the pilot could have deliberately chosen such a site. Remembering the account of the landing he had heard, Jim was sure that Mark hadn't chosen it. He must have been coming down toward the clearer section where Freddy's ship lay when the boy appeared on his screen. Only desperation to avoid a collision with the ferry could account for the location of Marks ship.

Jim couldn't believe now that Mark had lived through it. The landing on such terrain must have smashed most of the ship to splinters.

At fifty miles, there were more details. And things looked worse instead of better. There seemed to be no really good spot to land. Even in the seemingly smooth sections, there were deep holes and sharp bumps that stood out in the glaring black-and-white sunlight.

One spot in the level section looked as good as another, and the place Jim had originally chosen still was his best bet. He continued on down toward it. Nora flipped on the polarizing screen, hoping it would alter the appearance enough to give them more details, but he shook his head. It only made the seeing harder. She flipped it aside again.

Jim began to realize now that he wouldn't be able to make a final choice until the last five miles of the descent. It would leave no time for maneuvering, but it couldn't be helped. The slanting rays of the sunlight exaggerated heights by casting long shadows, but left hollows their normal size. If there had been any atmosphere to diffuse and soften the light, seeing wouldn't have been so bad. But here everything seemed cut out in hard, sharp lines of ink and chalk. There must have been grays down there, since reflected light would bounce into some of the shadows, but he couldn't detect it from this

126

height.

At twenty miles, it began forming a clearer pattern, and Jim could see that his proposed site was even rougher than he had thought. He slid his eyes across the screen, hunting. Nothing nearer Freddy's ship looked at all promising. The only area that seemed safe lay at least twenty miles further away.

He had no choice now. It had to be the site he'd picked or nothing. The ships couldn't continue maneuvering for any distance, and it was the only section within their reach. Jim began reeling out the change in course, toward the best spot in his chosen location, with no time to figure it accurately. There was nothing he could do but reach an approximation and trust to luck.

Poorhouse was having trouble following him closely enough, but the pilot seemed to get himself under control, and the *Oberth* began edging toward the other ships. Gantry's *Hohmann* seemed not to have come an inch closer or further during the whole descent.

Jim felt one of the passengers behind him, staring over his shoulder at the screen. He couldn't look back to see what fool had unbuckled the seat straps in such circumstances. He jerked his elbow back viciously. There was a pained gasp and the clutching pressure on his shoulder was suddenly gone.

There was the brief sound of a scuffle, and then Pierotti's voice sounded in low, quick words. "Okay, Jim. Got him strapped down!"

Jim's sudden anger subsided almost as quickly as it had come. He couldn't afford the emotion. And he couldn't entirely blame whoever it had been. There was an almost hypnotic fascination to the rugged harshness below, and a certain macabre beauty. At ten miles, the smooth section still seemed fairly safe. Jim noticed now that there was a break in the ground beyond it, where they might be able to base their huts safely. He began edging over a trifle. The cargo ship would have to land close enough for the cranes to swing the sections into place without too much hauling. But he couldn't come too close to the crevasse for fear the ground might crumble under the weight of the ship. About thirty feet from the edge would probably be best, leaving room beyond for the other two.

He hadn't called corrections, but Poorhouse started to imitate his maneuver. Gantry said something harshly, and the other pilot stopped his creep toward the edge. The *Hohmann* was moving down steadily, now letting Jim slip away for the first time. It wasn't hard to see why Gantry had won over his difficulties. The man's nerves were chilled steel and his thoughts were always ahead of the situation.

At five miles, they were moving fairly slowly. But it was Jim's final chance to change his mind. He caught a quick view of Freddy's ship, more than four miles away. It was tough, but there was nothing he could do to improve the situation. The ground directly below still looked like the best spot. Even from this height, it seemed as smooth as if it had been filled in.

Maybe it had been, Jim realized. He'd heard that fine dust could creep slowly under the pull of gravity, even without a wind to blow. If the section down there were smooth only because of such dust moving to fill the holes and cover irregularities, the legs of the ship would sink into it and might hit anything! There would be no way of knowing the depth, either. If they sank too far, the dust would make it impossible to move around outside the ship, even if the jets from the rockets blew it out of the way at first.

He had a picture of a deep split in the ground, filled in to fifty or a hundred feet with dust. But he put it out of his mind. It wasn't logical that there could be that much dust in any one spot on a world without winds to blow it into the hollows from a large surrounding area.

He called a quick warning of his suspicions into the microphone. They would have to come down slowly, unless there was some way of seeing what lay on the surface. Those last few feet would be even worse than he had thought. It was probably all solid rock, but they couldn't take chances.

At a mile up, Gantry grunted. "No dust. Cracks!"

Jim spotted the cracks then; there could have been no such signs if there had been dust to fill them in. They were fine lines, like the cracks in sun-baked mud. They probably had been caused by the changing heat and cold expanding and contracting the ground. None of them seemed wide enough to permit the big feet of the landing legs to sink, however.

Near the sharp break where Jim was heading, the cracks seemed thicker. He wondered whether it meant that the ledge there was rotten and ready to break apart completely under the ship. But it was too late to change now. Poorhouse was fairly close on the other side, without too much room for edging back. Jim had picked his spot as well as he could. From now on, he could only hope for reasonable luck. Most of the supplies would still be good, even if the ledge crumbled and threw the cargo ship over; there were only ten in the total crew of fifty here, and the ship hadn't been meant to take off into space again, anyhow. He was the logical one to risk it.

The low-range altimeter registered about a thousand feet. Jim snapped a quick look at the fuel gauge near it, remembering that he had no reserve tanks. In an emergency, the other two ships might draw on their return tanks. He had none. The needle registered near the bottom of the scale, but there seemed to be enough fuel for the landing.

Then they were five hundred feet up. Jim took a last look at the screen. He was positioned as well as he could be, with Poorhouse and Gantry spread out at about the right spacing.

The blast from the rocket hit the ground then, ending all visibility. That was something he'd expected, but it brought a tight knot into his stomach, all the same. The last few hundred feet — the trickiest ones-had to be handled blind. There was no way of looking through the hot splashing flame of his own exhaust as it bounced off the ground.

He kept his eyes on the altimeter with quick side glances at the screens that showed some indications of the ground beyond. The needle on the meter went down to fifty feet, and then was useless as the blast kicked up enough solid matter to trigger it. Twenty feet more, maybe.

The ship seemed to hover, but he knew it was still falling. He juggled the control, trying to sense the position of the ship and waiting for the first faint contact with the feeler leg. He'd have to react instantly to correct, if it failed to cut the blast automatically. And it seemed impossible that anything could stand the heat of that splashing exhaust.

The ship pitched faintly, and then again. He was so low that the surface beneath was affecting the blast, driving it up against the ship and acting like a strong wind under him.

But it gave him a clearer idea of his height. He eased up, with every nerve in his body straining to feel and read the faintest touch as he cut the blast slightly.

He was hardly moving. He eased up again, beginning to worry that he'd reached minimum speed too high above the ground.

Then a red light sprang up in front of him. The feeler leg had touched!

Abruptly, the blast cut off, just as he was about to snap it off manually. The feeler leg had worked. Now the springs in the landing legs coupled with the shock absorbers to soak up the last few bits of speed the ship possessed.

The *Goddard* sank another foot, bounced up slowly for an inch or so, and settled down to a firm, level position!

Chapter 19 - Rescue Party

THROUGH THE observation dome Jim could see the other two ships, both resting solidly on the rock below them. A quick check by radio showed no sign of injury to men or machines; even the fuel consumption had been satisfactory.

"Good." Gantry's voice showed quiet approval. "A fine job, Jim. I expected it."

His voice was muffled as he issued orders to his own crew; then he turned back to the microphone. "I'm having the tractor pulled out at once by its driver. Nobody else is to leave the ship until I give out work orders. Dr. Perez, Nora — you'll form a rescue party under Dr. Charkejian, since he probably knows lunar conditions best. Leave at once, and keep radio contact with Poorhouse. No needless risks. Jim, suppose you look over the terrain here while I report to Earth."

Jim had taken it for granted that he would help in the rescue attempt, but he realized Gantry had been right in his assignments. There was still no radio contact with the wrecked ferry as he buckled on his suit and headed outside, where Nora and the others were carrying a stretcher and supplies out to the little tractor. The machine looked like a small caterpillar-treaded tank with a plastic bubble on top, and it spouted out a cloud of steam as it crawled off at a few miles an hour.

Their chances for a rescue didn't look good. At this distance, there should have been some answer to their radio signals. Jim had been hoping that Mark might have joined Freddy, if he'd lived. The ferry was in better condition, and it was also better located for a rescue. Mark would have realized that and headed there. Now the lack of any response seemed to indicate the worst for both of them.

Jim tried to put the worry out of his mind and concentrate on his job. The ground around the ships seemed to be a shelf of solid rock, with only small shallow cracks. He nodded in satisfaction, and moved on to the crevasse he'd spotted. It began thirty feet from his ship. The rocky shelf seemed to have split apart, leaving a fissure nearly a hundred feet deep and three times as wide. At the bottom, the floor was fairly smooth, and there was even a slope that might be used for a road down it. Best of all, the rock was undercut near the bottom. It would offer fairly good shelter for their base, if it proved safe.

He studied the cargo ship. They'd have to guy the other side of it down to keep it from tipping, but the crane would be able to reach over into the fissure.

In the end, only the frame and base would be left of the ship, to mount the solar mirror for power and the antenna for contact with Earth. Nearly all the rest would be salvaged to build and equip the living quarters. Jim hated losing his only command, but it had always been planned that way.

He started back to report, just as he saw Gantry heading toward the airlock of the *Goddard*. Jim flicked on his personal radio. "Freddy? Or Mark?"

"No news yet," Gantry told him. "We're getting a lot of news from Earth, but most of it is politics." He shook his head, as if puzzled, and then smiled. "Don't worry about losing your ship, Jim. Poorhouse is third pilot, so you'll take over on the way back, no matter what happens. That was a perfect job you did. Now, what about conditions here?"

Jim began reporting as they filed through the airlock of the cargo ship and toward the control cabin.

"It's better than we expected from what we saw," Gantry decided when Jim had finished. "I'll have a couple of men test the edge of the fissure. Then we'll begin working on quarters. With only six weeks here to explore a whole world, we can't waste much time."

They reached the cabin, where Pierotti and Jonas were pressed close to the radio that was broadcasting from the relay station, with everyone else clumped around it tightly. There was something about the new plans under the internationalized setup, and Gantry stopped to listen. Then, before Jim could make sense of it, the interconnecting radio sounded, and Gantry reached for it, signaling for the other broadcast to be cut. "Just made contact with

132

the tractor again," Poorhouse reported. "They're near the ferry now. From what they can see, the airlock is buried and there's no way for them to break in. They don't have picks with them."

"All right, I'll send them from here," Gantry answered. He swung back to face Jim. "You're elected. Pick someone else, and get going. It's faster than having the tractor come back."

Jim nodded toward Jonas, and the older man was in his suit by the time the picks had been located and unpacked. The two started out at a trot that was easy to maintain in this low gravity, following the trail of the tractor. There was enough dust and small rubble to mark it, and it saved time to follow where Charkejian had already found a way.

"If the lock's sealed, how could Mark reach the boy?" Jonas asked suddenly.

Jim had been wondering about the same thing.

There was only one possible answer, and he didn't like it. It was hard to give up all hope.

The ground wasn't as rough as it had looked from the ship, or at least there was more clear space between the harsh, jagged-edged rocks. And it wasn't the sharp blacks and whites it had seemed. At closer view, there were all colors in the rocks, and shadings of light where the reflections illuminated the shadows. But it was tricky, and travel took most of their attention. There were fissures and small cracks everywhere. Without the erosion of rain and wind, the raw bones of the satellite had never been worn smooth, and the sharp lines of light and shadow made it seem even rougher.

They reached the top of the roughest section. Jonas pointed suddenly, and Jim turned to follow his motion.

Here, in a detour the tractor had taken to find better going, they were no more than a mile from Mark's ship. It stood across an impassable maze of cuts and rocky heights, at the top of another small peak. Jim swung the binoculars to his eyes, focusing them against his helmet visor, and then gasped.

There wasn't much left of the former third stage. Mark had apparently found the levelest section in a bad spot, but no place had been safe. The ship must have come down too fast, dropping on its motors and tanks. A jagged rock had cut through the whole lower section and through what was left of the hull, splitting the framework apart as if a wedge had been driven in. Girders were twisted and bent, and the control cabin was gaping open. It didn't need the dangling airlock door to show that there was no air in the ship, nor any chance of a man living in it.

But hanging outside was a rope ladder that led down to the surface. That could have only been unrolled after the ship had landed. It seemed impossible that Mark could have survived, but he must have.

"His only chance was at the ferry boat with Freddy," Jim decided, but there was little hope in his voice. He turned, dropping the binoculars back into their pouch, and headed up the trail, Jonas beside him.

Then they were suddenly around a curve and almost at the other ship.

The ferry must have tipped in landing, and had buried part of the control sphere, covering the airlock. Jim had been expecting that. But he hadn't expected the big metal sheet that had been bent to form a crude sled and now stood beside the little ship. On it was piled a miscellaneous collection of supplies — food, water, small oxygen tanks, and other things.

Nora had come up to Jim, taking one of the picks. "That's right," she said dully. "Mark made it here. He brought two big oxygen tanks, too, and coupled them to the valves on the ferry. But he couldn't get in."

"What about Freddy?" Jonas asked her. She shrugged helplessly. "We don't know. No answer."

They fell to work on the rocks and rubble around the lock. It was mostly soft stuff that gave quickly to the picks. The others shoveled it aside as Jim and Nora dug. They had to go deep enough to get under the lock, with enough room to swing it open. It was back-breaking work, particularly since too much effort tended to make them bounce from the surface.

But finally Jim's pick dragged out a bigger lump of rock, and he could swing the outer part of the lock open. There was barely room enough for him to crowd in behind Perez and Nora.

Jim snapped his helmet open briefly as the inner lock opened.

The air was foul, but it was breathable, apparently. Then he saw Freddy.

The boy lay stretched out on the lower part of the control room. He seemed to have shrunken until the bones stood out from his skin, and his lips were cracked. If he were breathing, it was too shallow to show.

Perez twisted the valve on the air supply. They could waste it now, and it cleared some of the thickness out. He lifted one of the thin arms and nodded. "Shock. Fix the plasma while I work on him." He ran a needle into the thin arm and injected something quickly, turning to prepare something else.

"He's alive?" Jim asked.

"I haven't time to find out," Perez answered. "When something looks like this kind of shock reaction, it's the same as death unless you get antishock stuff into him fast. Ah!"

He inserted the needle while Nora held up the plasma bottle.

Abruptly the chest quivered and a darkened tongue came out to lick across the cracked lips. Perez moistened a sponge and added something to it before placing it over the boy's mouth. "Thirst and partial starvation," he said. "That and fright. Give me a hand getting a suit on him, Jim."

Apparently the oxygen Mark must have coupled into the lines had been enough. But Freddy hadn't known how to manage his food and water, from the looks of the place.

"Clock's ruined," Perez said suddenly.

Jim looked, and he could see that the chronometer had apparently been ruined in the landing. Then it hit him. Freddy had been here with no way to tell time for all the days of waiting! He must have thought the rescue overdue a hundred times. He had a reason for going somewhat mad with hysterical fear, eventually — and the evidence here indicated such hysteria. Locked in, helpless, and with no idea of how long . . .

"Will he live now, do you think?"

Perez shook his head. "I don't know. That was a pretty advanced case of shock — the kind a man goes into before death. Of course, with these new drugs there's a chance. Wait, don't close the suit yet."

There was more plasma to be injected, as well as an intravenous of something else. Perez timed it carefully, and finally fed Freddy a small quantity of water.

That brought more reaction than they had expected. The eyes flickered open and Freddy's mouth worked painfully. "Jim!" he gasped. Something that might have been meant for a smile touched his lips, and then he was unconscious again.

"All right, zip him up," Perez ordered. He was putting supplies away hastily. "At least his mind seems clear. It gives us a fifty-fifty chance."

Nora and Charkejian took the stretcher and carried Freddy to the tractor, while the driver called the ships. She looked inquiringly at Jim, but he shook his head. There wasn't room on the tractor for him and Jonas. "I've got to see what happened to Mark," Jim told her.

She nodded reluctantly and climbed onto the tractor, leaving him alone with Jonas. The older man put a hand on his shoulder. "Don't count on anything," he warned.

The warning wasn't needed. Jim could recognize that Mark's time must have run out long before. The oxygen tanks that were coupled to the ferry and those abandoned on the sled showed that Mark hadn't expected to live.

Too many feet had ruined any trail near the ferry, but he finally found signs further on, heading back into the rocky ground toward the wreck of the pilot's ship. Silently, Jim and Jonas followed them. The trail led on for a mile, and then it began heading up toward the top of one of the little peaks, to disappear among the harder rock. But the destination was plain by then.

There was a sort of ledge a few feet from the very top, and Mark had seated himself there. At his back and to his left, a small projection rose up to the height of his shoulders, forming a sort of throne for him. It had left him in a position to see nearly all of Dewey Bay. The ferry and his rocket were within his view, and beyond, over the horizon, there was the great disk of Earth shining on him.

He was dead, of course. The open valve on his helmet showed that he had chosen to die quickly, when the air in his suit began to grow thick and stale. But his face was frozen in the same smile Jim had seen so often, and he was staring up at the Earth with no sign of regrets.

He'd left his final words, too. There was a sharp piece of metal in his hand, and scratched into the rock of the cliff were two lines:

PRIVATE PROPERTY
This World Claimed for Humanity!

Chapter 20 - New Worlds

THE PASSENGER GLOBE of the *Goddard* was trembling faintly from the work of the men who were tearing out the cargo tank to use as huts. Jim sat in it, removing the official papers he would need. But his eyes were out on the plain beyond.

Jonas slipped in quietly behind him, and also looked across the lunar landscape to the place where they'd left Mark in the place he'd chosen for himself. The pilot had been the first man to walk on the surface of this satellite, and it had seemed fitting that he should remain on it.

"I suppose he'll be the greatest of the Moon's heroes," Jonas said at last. "They'll have his words engraved all over, and statues of him on every corner. I guess he'd like that."

Jim nodded. Most of his grief was gone by now. It was hard to feel anguish over a man who hadn't regretted what had happened to him, and he was sure that Mark had somehow died happy. "Any news on Freddy?" he asked.

"Not yet, since Perez is keeping him under drugs. We should hear soon." Jonas sighed and sank down into one of the seats. "What a pilot the kid will make, if he learns a little discipline. There was nothing wrong with his landing, Nora tells me — just a bad rock. In five years, with the colony here . . ."

"A colony in five years?" Jim asked. He'd heard more talk while he had pitched in to help set up the living quarters down in the crevasse on his return, but he'd discounted that as part of the same wild dreams he had heard already too often on the ship. Now, coming from Jonas, it began to take on more than the value of idle chatter.

Jonas stared back at him in surprise. "Haven't you heard any of the news, Jim?"

He switched on the radio to the relay station broadcast without waiting for an answer. The words of some announcer came in promptly, but at first they had no meaning. Then, as Jonas began filling in, Jim sat up in his seat, trying to digest what he'd heard. It was incredible enough, even without the extraordinary speed at which it had been accomplished.

The committee appointed by the World Congress to regulate the internationalization of space included some of the best minds in all countries, and they'd already covered an amazing amount of ground. It was no mere figurehead group, but men who obviously meant to make sure that space was developed properly, and with no strings attached. More amazing, both the Combine and Alliance seemed perfectly willing to go along with the arrangement.

"But why?" Jim asked. "They fought to keep each other out of space, and they wrangled over the stations! Why all this?"

Jonas shrugged. "It's a complicated story, Jim, though I got advance warnings that something like this might be in the wind. I suppose you could say that the world is growing up and learning to co-operate, just as you've been doing. Maybe that's part of it, and I'd like to think so. But I suspect the real reason is that there was no other solution possible. They had to come to this, though it took a lot of slow juggling by President Andrews and Peter Chiam to bring things around to a level where they could try it."

"But they both lose space this way!" Jim protested. "Maybe the people as a whole gain it, but it gets out of their control."

"They can't control it anyhow, and they've found it out," Jonas said. "They don't dare let space stay a national affair. They've had too much trouble even with the stations. And out here, they can't afford to police a whole planet. But that's what they'd have to do. There's no real value to them worth fighting for in space, but things would get out of hand, just the same. They can't extend their sphere of power out here without the strength to back it up — and they literally can't afford that. Space had to be taken out of their hands, and we're just lucky that Andrews and Chiam could see it and still see the need to get out here."

It was hard to accept the facts, but they fitted. Any other system would have meant the trouble with the stations all over again, but worse and more expensive. And now maybe even the dangers of the stations could be ended. A tiny, international missile supply on the Moon wouldn't be enough to ruin the Earth, but it could knock out any station that tried to begin aggressive actions. In time, the people might realize the value of space without its dangers.

"But colonies in five years — " Jim began doubtfully.

"Not in five years! Now! When we leave here six weeks from now, five men are going to stay and work on the base for the next trip. And more will stay then, and so on. We'll have a hundred men based here in a year, growing their own air and part of their food in tanks."

And finally some enthusiasm began to hit Jim as he listened and discussed. It wouldn't be easy. At first, the scientific value of the trips would have to pay the way, together with what could be made from films, lectures and every other means that could be handled by a company Jonas was planning. Building ships that could use Earth's air as a brake to slow them for a return to the station would help to cut down the huge cost enormously. And already one of the chemists was laying out a program to have fuel plants working by solar energy and using materials — fortunately all common basic ones — within the next five years. Once that was done, the trips would be cheap enough for the colony to begin a true growth.

"And men will come out here, Jim," Jonas finished. "What they will do and how they'll live will remain for the future, just as it did when America was first settled. But somehow, this world won't be useless when it's really opened up. I've been thinking of settling down here myself."

They were still discussing it as they went down from the rocket and out onto the plain below. Then Jim saw Nora heading toward him, and turned toward her. She began running as she recognized him, calling over the radio in her suit.

"Freddy's conscious, Jim. He's going to be all right!"

The report was spreading all over a minute later. Freddy had sat up finally, and his mind had been clear, though he was still terribly weak. He'd managed to say hello to his father over the radio. It would still be several days before he could have company, but he was going to recover.

Jim felt the final weight lift from him as he realized that the rush and drive of the trip hadn't been wasted.

Then he looked around at the unfamiliar landscape around

him. Nothing that could get men here would have been a waste, he decided.

Men hadn't even begun to explore it yet. That would start in the six weeks remaining before their return, and would go on for years as they learned to know this new world. But already it didn't seem so strange. Jim wondered whether any world would seem strange very long to the men who would go out to them. They wouldn't stop here; there was the cloud-wrapped mystery of Venus and the proof of some kind of life on Mars to drive them on. In the future to come, there might be no limits to the places and worlds men might find.

But for now, this was enough.

Then he grinned and glanced down at Nora.

"We'll have to spend the next five years piloting for others, I guess," he told her. "But after that, maybe Freddy will be ready to take over. This wouldn't be a bad place to settle down, do you think?"

She smiled back at him. "No, Jim. I can't think of a better place."

They stood quietly then, studying the new world that was to be their home.

THE END

If you enjoyed this book, look for others like it at Thunderchild Publishing: http://www.ourworlds.net/thunderchild/

Made in the USA
Middletown, DE
06 June 2017